IN TOO DEEP

THE PORTAL KEEPERS
BOOK ONE

LEAH R CUTTER

KNOTTED ROAD PRESS

ALSO BY LEAH R CUTTER

Urban/Contemporary Fantasy Series
The Witch's Progress

Circle of Air

Circle of Fire

Circle of Water

Circle of Earth

Seattle Trolls

The Changeling Troll

The Princess Troll

The Fairy-Bridge Troll

The Troll-Demon War

The Troll-Human War

The Troll-Troll War

The Shadow Wars Trilogy

The Raven and the Dancing Tiger

The Guardian Hound

War Among the Crocodiles

The Clockwork Fairy Kingdom

The Clockwork Fairy Kingdom

The Maker, the Teacher, and the Monster

The Dwarven Wars

The Cassie Stories

Poisoned Pearls

Tainted Waters

Spoiled Harvest

Bloodied Ice

The Chronicles of Franklin

Franklin Versus The Popcorn Thief

Franklin Versus The Soul Thief

Franklin Versus The Child Thief

Epic Fantasy Series

The Fallen Elves

Ruins of the Gods

Stairs of the Gods

Cities of the Gods

Graves of the Gods

Houses of the Dead

Houses Divided

Houses Fallen

Houses Reborn

Forgotten Gods

A Wind Blown Torment

A Stone Strewn Clash

A Sea Washed Victory

The Tanesh Empire Trilogy

The Glass Magician

The Desert Heart

The Ghost Dog

Mysteries

The Purloined Letter Opener

The Tell-Tale Heart Pin

Dancer in Darkness

Trophy Hunters

The Alvin Goodfellow Case Files

The Rabbit Mysteries

The Shredded Veil Mysteries

Mystery, Crime, and Mayhem

Science Fiction

The Long Run

Project Nemesis

Project Nyx

Project Tisiphone

Project Persephone

War of the Allied Worlds

The Complete Labors of Darius Linard

Huli Intergalactic: Science/Space Fantasy

Origins

The Strawberry Girl

ONE

SAM WAS PUTTING clamps on the dove-tailed corners of a drawer when it happened.

It always filled Sam with a sense of pride when the carved wooden corners fit together just so, despite putting together hundreds of drawers and cabinets in the woodworking shop over the past ten years.

She'd already applied the clamps and was wiping away one last drop of glue when suddenly, everything started glowing.

What the hell? Who was playing with the lights?

Sam took a step back from her work bench and looked up.

The bright shop lights still hung from the ceiling, buzzing and obnoxious fluorescent bulbs hanging in wire cages so they wouldn't accidentally be broken by flying wood chips. A strange black mist obscured them.

Or rather, a mist *had* been covering them. It was now dissolving away. It reminded Sam of a clip she'd seen of an old fashioned 8 millimeter film burning. The black bubbled and withdrew in circles, each running into the next until all the lights were clear, shining like sunlight on a spring day. Despite the strangeness of the situation, Sam wasn't scared.

The regular scent of fresh pine and the chemical smell of colored paint blasted against her, as if someone had just turned on a fan. Sam shook her head, fighting off the urge to sneeze.

The light in the shop increased in intensity, as though the ceiling had just lowered, placing the lights right on top of her.

She shook her head again, wiping her eyes with the back of her hand.

Had someone slipped something into her water bottle? This wasn't some sort of hangover or reaction to something. It was only Tuesday. She hadn't been out drinking the night before.

She turned to Juan at the next workbench, but he didn't appear to notice that anything was wrong. He continued to run his fingers over the shelves he was working on, using the highest grit sandpaper whenever he detected a blemish.

Sam turned back to her own workbench. The wood there continued to glow, whiter and brighter than she'd ever seen it before.

An inkling of what was happening shook Sam to her core. Her stomach hollowed out and her throat was suddenly dry.

She wanted to deny it. This couldn't be happening. Not to her. And certainly not while she was at work. She needed to get out of here. Now.

The drawer on her workbench captured her attention.

Sam knew she shouldn't. But she couldn't help herself. She reached out and stroked her fingers across the smooth wood, following the grain.

Though it had been a long while since that board had come from the forest, the wood still spoke of the trees it had known, the brilliance of the summer sun, the fierceness of the winter frost. Sam found herself sinking deeper, feeling the roughness of the bark that had protected the tree this wood had come from, how good it had felt to dig deep into the earthy loam and anchor one's self, listening to songs created by wind whistling through branches and pine needles.

With great effort, Sam snatched her hand away as if it had been burned.

It was one of the first things her parents had taught her about magic: you couldn't go in too deep.

If she had let herself sink further, she could have transported herself there, to that forest, to the exact location where the tree had come from.

Without any portal set up ahead of time to bring her back.

Sam didn't remember the first time she'd been told that she was a witch, that she came from a family of strong witches. She'd started using magic before she could walk. However, like most practitioners, she didn't have enough power to do serious damage either to herself or to anyone around her.

That had apparently changed.

Grandma Starling had just died. Instead of passing

her power on to Sam's brother Morgan, as everyone had expected, her grandmother had remained as contrary as always up to the very end. It look as though she'd passed it to Sam.

No. This was *not* supposed to happen. Sam wasn't really part of the family anymore, the black sheep who could barely read and who worked a blue collar job in the trades instead of being some lawyer or doctor. Or even an investment banker, like her brother.

She glanced around the shop again. The wood continued to glow, calling to her, longing to tell her its stories, but it was getting easier to ignore it. The smells of the workshop faded, though harsh scent of varnish continued to tickle the back of her throat. Sounds returned—the whine of the chop saw loud in the corner, a Mexican love song crooning from the radio on Pedro's bench, the chatter of the two men across from her.

Sam shivered, both too warm and too cold. Goose-bumps chased each other across her shoulders and down her back.

What was she supposed to do now?

A feeling of menace washed over her, coming from the right.

Slowly, Sam turned and looked.

It was Darren. The new guy. The one who'd given her the creeps from day one.

He was staring at her.

As she looked, that same black film that had appeared to cover the lights now burned off Darren, revealing that he wasn't exactly human. His auburn hair dissolved and his skin brightened, until it was glowing

4

red. Liquid black eyes stared out above an ugly snout. Puke green horns grew out of his forehead, and claws the same nasty color tipped his fingers. Muscles upon muscles rippled across his broad, bare chest.

He'd always worn too much of that awful men's body spray. Now, that scent mingled with the stench of moldy leaves, setting her eyes to watering again. Ugh.

Darren, or whatever the hell his name actually was, had just been revealed as a creature from the netherworlds.

And now that Sam had power, *real* power that she had no idea how to use, he was going to try to steal it from her. Probably by killing her.

Well, shit.

SAM KNEW she couldn't go out to the parking lot and drive away. Darren would catch her there. If she asked Juan or Pedro to come with, they'd just end up getting killed.

But she had to get out of here, before Darren decided that he could justify a super-high body count and just kill all the guys in the shop in order to get to her. Most of whom were like uncles and brothers to her.

She couldn't endanger them that way. She left the workshop, going into the hallway, then down to the employee breakroom. Through habit, she automatically clocked out.

They were a union shop. All of them took pride in being paid the hours they worked and nothing more.

The breakroom may have been a mistake. There were no windows in here. No obvious natural portal, either. And she wasn't desperate enough to touch one of Pedro's tamales, made by his *abuela*, though the corn husk might give her a place to go to, a way of escaping.

Pedro would never forgive her for destroying one of those. They were the last of the batch his *abuela* had sent him before she'd died.

As Sam spun around to leave, Darren showed up, his bulky shoulders brushing the edges of the doorframe. He closed the door behind him.

The sound of the lock being thrown was ominous.

Sam skirted past the table in the center of the room to the far corner, opposite the door. What could she use to stop this beast? Throw the microwave at him? It was only the fifteenth of May, so there wasn't anything truly noxious in the fridge, not yet. It regularly got cleaned on the first of the month, so Juan's forgotten and moldy sandwiches and Sam's equally moldy left-over fries wouldn't become their own lifeform.

The table was cheap laminate. When they'd tried to have solid wood furniture in here, no one had been satisfied with it being good enough. The chairs were all brightly colored plastic, heavy duty enough to support the weight of the bigger guys like Saul, but none of them would make a good weapon.

"Thank you for coming in here, for making this easier," Darren said. He voice still sounded reedy, like it was coming from a tall, thin, twenty-two-year-old white guy with mommy issues.

"You aren't going to take me," Sam said heatedly.

Even on such a non-human face, Darren's confusion was evident. "You didn't come in here so I could kill you?"

"Do I look like I want to be killed? Like I'm ready to die?" Sam asked heatedly.

Darren paused, looking her over. Sam wasn't sure what those dismal eyes of his saw.

Her hair was raven black, cut short and layered. She'd been promised a cute pixie cut, but it hadn't turned out that way. Problem was, Sam wasn't a pixie. Or petite. She was average height, five foot seven, and she'd been working in the trades for most of her adult life, which meant she had broad shoulders, strong muscular arms, and hands that had been abused by both tools and chemicals. She'd been told she looked like Grandma Starling, with a perfectly round head, chubby cheeks, a nose that melted onto her face, thick lips and a wide smile.

Or at this point, a pointed glare.

Darren responded by showing off his own set of pointed teeth. She doubted it was any sort of friendly grin.

"You look tasty," he said. "The power all on the edges of you. Easy to lick off."

"Watch it with the inappropriate comments," Sam warned. Though who would she report it to? Ron, the shop steward, couldn't stop this monster any better than she could.

"Say your prayers," Darren said. "And prepare to meet your creator."

Sam couldn't help but roll her eyes at the smugness of his comments. Really, who said such crap?

Unfortunately, she didn't see a way out. He was going to steal all the power she'd just been gifted. Warlocks, the oath breakers, did that to witches.

Sure, she'd been taught some self-defense.

However, no one had believed that she'd ever need it, at least not against a magical foe. She had never been the one destined for power. Morgan had been the one who'd taken all the lessons, had the private tutors, leaned how to deal with fangs and horns.

Sam had been diagnosed with dyslexia at a young age, and as far as her parents had been concerned, that put her out of the running for any sort of magical greatness.

Maybe she could lure Darren to the far side of the breakroom and escape out the door? It had been locked from the inside. It would only take a few seconds for her to undo it.

Then he rushed her.

Sam sprinted to the side, barely avoiding being swiped by one long claw.

Damn, he was fast.

She couldn't turn her back on him. She didn't have two seconds to unlock the door.

Sam feinted left, then ran right. Darren fell for it, and so they circled the table in the center of the room again.

"Surely you can do better than that," Darren commented.

What, was he trying to goad her?

"I can do this all day," Sam replied cheekily.

"No, you cannot," Darren said. He abruptly shoved the table at her.

Sam barely got out of the way of the cheap laminate slamming against the counter at the back of the room. The table cracked and buckled under the pressure.

Then Darren was on her. Claws cut her biceps where he held her. The stench of his rot made her eyes water. She struggled, bringing up a sharp knee, but he easily avoided it.

His hot breath steamed against her skin. Black eyes bore into hers, not an abyss that she wanted to delve into. Saliva dripped from the front fangs of his snout.

"You are mine," he intoned.

He removed one clawed hand from her shoulder, up to her neck, then started squeezing the life out of her.

Sam beat at the steel-like arms holding her up, though all she did was bruise her own fists. She clawed at the leathery skin ineffectually. At least one sharp kick landed on his knee, but she was rapidly losing air.

"No!" she tried to scream through her bruised throat. It came out as a bare squeak.

Probably just as well. Anyone coming to save her would end up dead too.

The room was starting to dim. All that bright light streaming away. She frantically tried to remember a spell or some magical trick to get Darren to release her. Her thoughts circled around and around the fact that she couldn't breathe.

And that this asshole was going to get all her power before she'd even had a chance to use it.

CHAPTER

THREE

SAM CONTINUED TO STRUGGLE. She couldn't breathe. Tears blinding her. All that power she'd inherited was starting to drain away.

A cool shiver of wind brushed against Sam's left shoulder, reviving her slightly. She heard the words, "Pardon me."

It took Sam a few moments to process what she'd just seen. A fist had come out of nowhere and *slammed* itself up against Darren's lower jaw, snapping his head back.

Darren dropped Sam as he took a few staggering steps back. Sam barely managed to land on her feet, bent over, trying not to vomit.

"You are damaging something that I've sworn to protect," came the haughty words.

Sam struggled to breathe through her bruised throat. Tears sprang to her eyes when she coughed.

"Wait," she tried to croak. *Don't kill him on the property* was what she wanted to say.

The paperwork would be horrendous. And the guys would never forgive her for all the blood in the breakroom.

The tall man (though it wasn't a man, any more than Darren was) responded with a sharp backhand across Darren's snout.

Ow. Given the way Darren was now shaking his head, that had to have hurt.

The lights were brightening again. Sam gave a painful gasp as the damned elf (yes, that was an elf, no doubt about it) drew a particularly pretty sword out of nowhere. Of course it glowed with the power of a thousand suns, making her eyes water more.

"Don't," she managed to get out.

The elf glanced back at her, giving Darren the opportunity to get in a solid punch to the elf's mid-section.

It was now the elf's turn to stagger back a few steps. Anger radiated off the elf, strong enough to heat Sam's cheeks.

"Don't kill him," Sam finally managed to say as the elf rounded on the monster in front of him.

Though she didn't know this elf at all, or even really elves in general, she could still see the frustration across his tight shoulders, the way he set his clean-shaven jaw.

"Very well, mistress," he said through gritted teeth.

Instead of ramming Darren through with the sword, the elf feinted left, right, then sliced up in the air. With a dramatic flair, he brought the flat of the sword down on the monster's head.

Bright fireworks went off, blinding Sam. When she

managed to clear her tear-filled eyes, Darren was gone. A lingering aftereffect glow remained for a few moments, only to quickly dissipate. The smell of magic, cool and lemony, washed over Sam.

"You didn't just vanish him, did you?" Sam demanded, rounding on the elf. "You can't just vanish people."

Making someone disappear for good from the earthly plane caused far too many issues. Police would eventually get involved. Sam couldn't even imagine what her shop steward would say.

"No, I didn't just 'vanish' him, as you so colloquially call it," the elf replied, disdain dripping from every word. "I sent him back to his plane of origin. He can surely make it back here on his own."

Sam nodded, though the movement hurt her bruised throat. "And his car?" she demanded.

The elf's eyes grew wide for a moment, then narrowed. "Very well," he said. He closed his eyes and raised his nose, like some sort of exquisitely bred hound searching for a scent. "It's done."

Sam didn't bother asking where the elf had sent Darren's car. Would serve Darren right if it appeared directly above him on whatever hell plane he'd come from.

"We need to go," the elf told Sam. "Madam Starling has passed, and against all our wishes, chose *you* for an heir."

"Wasn't my idea," Sam replied, grimacing. What was she supposed to do with all this magical power?

She was now a target, and would be for a while,

until she learned how to use it, to just make people vanish, as the elf had. Or maybe other things. She didn't know for certain.

Damn it! No one had ever bothered to train her at all.

She finally took a good look at the elf. He was perfectly beautiful, as all of his kind were. Tall, maybe six foot four, with the same raven dark hair that she sported. Only his was exquisitely coiffed. She bet he had more hair products on his bathroom shelves than she'd owned over the course of her thirty-five years.

While Sam's own white skin had a brown hue to it, the elf was pale and pink, like porcelain. He had a long, angular face absolutely made for looking haughty and superior. The primary differences between an elf and a human were in the fluted, pointed ears with extra, frilly skin around the edges that hung like ornate doorhandles on either side of his head, the cat-like golden eyes that were of course glaring at her, and the sharp, pointed teeth that all creatures from the nether planes shared.

He was dressed in a fine black suit, tailored to fit the slim creature in front of her perfectly. His white shirt practically glowed against it. He wore a golden tie (that matched his eyes) with white and red stripes running diagonally across it.

He looked like a high-powered lawyer who only took clients who could afford to dress better than he could—a very exclusive group.

An abrupt knock on the breakroom door interrupted whatever the elf was about to say to Sam next.

She walked over and unlocked the door, letting Juan in.

"You okay?" he said, glancing at her, then scowling at the elf. Juan was about the same height as Sam, but add thirty pounds of muscle and fierce protectiveness. He always wore short-sleeved shirts over the wife-beater T-shirts that his wife bleached to eye-searing whiteness. Today's overshirt was cotton, with a pattern of faded gold, red, and green checks. He looked, and acted, like everybody's Dad in the shop. Sam wasn't sure of his age, as his black hair was just starting to turn white and his tanned skin wasn't too wrinkled. She'd guess in his fifties, though, based on his conversations.

"My grandmother—Grandma Starling—has died," Sam said truthfully enough. "This is her lawyer."

It was as good of an excuse as any for why this strange man was here, in the breakroom with her, with the door locked.

Juan, though, was staring at her throat. "He do this?" he asked darkly.

"No, no," Sam said. The guys in the shop much more protective than any of her biological family. She grimaced. "That was Darren."

"I'll make sure his last paycheck is mailed to him," Juan promised.

"Thank you," Sam said. She knew that was for the best. If Darren ever showed his face at the shop again he'd get his ass kicked, particularly once the story got out that he'd attacked her. And even a creature from the nether planes might be challenged with a half dozen pissed-off human fighters.

Particularly since she knew the guys like Pedro and Ron wouldn't fight fair, and would instead start their attack with the knives they always carried.

Juan gave Sam a once-over. She self-consciously fidgeted. Juan's dark eyes wouldn't miss much, not the way her throat was red and already bruising, the tear tracks down her cheeks, or even the scratches on her arms from Darren's claws.

"Did Darren do that?" Juan asked, nodding toward the busted up breakroom table.

"Yes," Sam said.

"I'll get that taken out of his pay before it's sent to him, then," Juan said. He seemed to be looking for something, anything, to make her feel better.

"I'm fine," Sam assured him. "I'll be fine."

"You need to go be with family, now," he said firmly. He nodded to the elf. "You take good care of her, get her to the right people."

The elf's eyes widened. Sam sniggered to herself. Old elfie there probably hadn't ever had a human order him around before.

Humility was good for the soul. Not that she was certain the elves had souls. Some of those on the nether worlds claimed they did. Others proudly disdained them.

"I will take her to the rest of the family," the elf promised. He gave Sam a pointed look.

There was a part of Sam that stubbornly wanted to clock back in, to work the rest of her shift. While she suspected that the elf wouldn't allow it, she knew that

Juan would absolutely forbid it. Might even have a word with Ron to make sure that she left early.

"We'll take my Jeep," Sam said, knowing that the elf would much rather just open a portal to the estate.

"You sure?" Juan asked, still looking concerned.

"Yeah. Driving out to Ravenswood will help clear my head," she said. And it would, because she was going to take the top off the Jeep before they headed out.

It wasn't just because she wanted to see if the wind would mess with the elf's hair. Really. She also wanted that cool breeze to keep her grounded.

Because things had just gotten really strange, and chances were, this wasn't the half of it.

CHAPTER

FOUR

"So what do I call you?" Sam asked the elf as she finished folding the roof of her bright yellow Jeep back into the storage compartment behind the rear seats. The May afternoon sky was the clearest, cleanest blue she'd ever seen. It would be a little chilly without the top on. However, the Jeep came with an awesome heater.

"Alanthin Himladhon," he said grandly, though he still was looking dubiously at the Jeep.

"I'm just going to call you Al, all right?" Sam asked as she swung herself up into the driver's seat. "Hop in."

Al glared at her. "That isn't my name."

"You can call me Sam," she said in response. "You don't need to call me madam, or mistress, or whatever other title they told you to use."

Al continued to glare at her as he made his way to the passenger side of the Jeep. "You don't actually have to drive this, this, monstrosity," he said as he climbed in. "We could just use a portal to get to Madam Stirling's estate. Though I suppose it's now your estate."

Sam shook her head, wincing as the movement aggravated her sore neck. She was not looking forward to the snide comments that Morgan would give her for not being able to protect herself. Or her mother's guilt trips for not visiting Grandma Starling as well as the rest of them more often. Or any of the other thousand cuts that her biological family would give her while she was with them.

"Do I have to take it? The estate?" Sam asked as she threw the Jeep into gear. That was one of the reasons why she got this particular Jeep—because it had a manual version, which made it better for climbing dirt and gravel roads in the mountains surrounding Seattle.

Not that she'd gone hiking very often the previous summer. Time had gotten away from her, particularly when she'd been trying to make up with her now ex-boyfriend, Ethan. He'd never liked hiking or camping all that much. Just one of the many differences that had driven them apart after three years.

Al looked so shocked at her statement Sam gave herself a half-dozen points on whatever score card they had going between them.

"What—why—of course you have to take it!" Al finally sputtered. "You're now the guardian of the Choowe portal!"

Sam sighed as she pulled out of the parking lot of the woodworking shop and onto the busy street. It would take them about thirty minutes to drive from the Sodo neighborhood of Seattle to Ravenswood, where her grandmother's estate—her estate—lay.

"As we all know, I wasn't supposed to get Grandma

Starling's magic," Sam said, turning the corner smoothly. Everything seemed so much easier with the power. It wasn't humming in her blood, but she could definitely feel something different. The patterns of the cars in front of her were obvious, which cars were going to turn which way. She felt herself sliding through traffic, frictionless.

"Do you know what happened? Why she chose me at the last minute?" Sam continued.

Al was quiet for long enough that Sam glanced over at him. He had those thin lips of his pressed together, as if holding back commentary.

"Well?" Sam said, insistent.

"It may not have just been her choice," Al admitted after a few moments. "The portal itself may have decided that you were the better candidate."

Sam blinked, surprised. She focused on the cars in front of her instead of saying anything. Finally, she couldn't hold the words at bay any longer.

"Why the ever living *fuck* would the Choowe portal choose me? And not Morgan?" Sam said. The words kept coming, even though she knew she should just shut her mouth. "Morgan's *always* been the chosen one. He's the one everyone assumed was destined for greatness. He's the one who received all the training, and would have known how to deal with Darren back there."

"Who?" Al asked.

"Darren. That nether beast," Sam said. "Don't try to distract me," she added. "Why me?"

"I don't know," Al said quietly.

She heard the words even over the loud wind

blowing through the Jeep. She glanced over at Al. He gave her a shrug.

Of course, his hair was still perfect. She was just going to have to try harder. Too much traffic ahead right now for her to get her speed up. Maybe later.

"So tell me why exactly you came to find me," Sam said, her resentment at having always been second-best under control again.

"I am the representative from the elvish realm, assigned to guard the human side of the Choowe portal," Al said.

"Huh," was all Sam had to say as she swung out of her lane to pass the dually truck towing a large boat. "For how long?"

"How long have I been the assigned guardian? Or how long is my assignment?" Al asked.

He had one long, thin hand out on the dashboard, bracing himself as Sam swung back into the lane, out of oncoming traffic.

She nearly snorted at him. They hadn't been in any danger. Her skin tingled with the power that she'd been gifted. She'd always been good with traffic, but now she knew without a doubt where the corners of her vehicle were, how the cars around her would shift forward and back.

"Both," she said.

"I've been the guardian of the Choowe gate since Madam Starling inherited it," Al admitted.

That meant he'd been around for the last sixty-odd years. Curious that she'd never seen him before. Then again, she'd only met representatives from the elven realm twice. Once, when she'd been eleven and had snuck into a meeting that she wasn't supposed to hear, and the second time as she'd been leaving from one of the many disastrous Sunday dinners that she'd been required to attend.

The dinners ended when she'd finally paid her parents back the money they'd loaned her to buy her condo. After that, they hadn't been able to call the tune or pull her strings as much.

She honestly had to wonder if her mother had been the one to talk to Grandma Starling about giving her magic to Sam, just to bring her back into the family. Though she doubted that her mother cared that much about Sam.

"Since Grandma Starling's passed her power onto me, will you stay the guardian of the portal?" Sam asked. She could imagine that Al would be trying his damnedest to get out of the position, now that she'd been assigned for the human plane.

"I don't know," Al said primly.

"Do you have a choice?" Sam asked. She really knew very little about the elves, besides the fact that they were pretty, as well as stuck up. However, they were one of the few friendly denizens of the netherworlds. And not even all elves were friendly. If she was remembering correctly, there were three types of elves: high elves, which surely Al was a representative of, the wood elves who were fairly neutral, and the dark elves, who were decidedly unfriendly.

The sigh that Al gave was quite impressive. It was so dramatic he might even score points against an emo thirteen-year-old girl. Not that she was tempted to say that to him.

"My wishes do not matter," he said. "I will follow the will of the High Council."

"Of course you will," Sam said. Just what she needed. A pouting elf as her counterpart.

However, the next one the council sent, because she was certain they'd send someone else, wouldn't necessarily be any better.

"So what exactly is it that you do?" Sam asked after another few minutes. They were getting off the one-laned road and back into regular traffic again.

"I protect the Choowe portal on the human side from those who would use it for ill will," Al replied. He sounded as if he were reading from a text book. "And I protect the human guardian."

"I don't need a bodyguard," Sam said hotly. "I can take care of myself."

"You need a protector," Al said firmly. "You've already shown that."

"Fine," Sam said. She glanced to her left, checking traffic and her blind spot before she changed lanes.

Funny, her throat didn't hurt as much as it had. When they pulled up at a stoplight, she pushed herself up and checked it out in the rearview mirror.

The bruises were already yellowed and fading.

Was that from the power she'd been gifted? If so, that was a pretty cool side effect she hadn't been expecting.

"Did you put some kind of healing spell on me?" Sam asked as the light turned green.

"No, why would I do that?" Al said, sounding offended.

"I don't know. Because some netherworld entity had just tried to choke me to death?" Sam said.

"As you can tell, you're already healing yourself," Al said with a negligent wave of his well-manicured hand.

Sam had to agree with his assessment. By the time she met up with her family, maybe most of the bruises would be gone. That would mean at least one less fault that her brother or mother could throw up in her face.

If she could only be that lucky the rest of the time she had to be with them.

FIVE

THE STARLING ESTATE in Ravenswood was off the main road, heading out of town. Not that there was much of a town, per se. Just a stop sign with a tiny local convenience store on one side, the volunteer fire department building on the other, and undeveloped woodlands after that.

Everything was still so green. The ends of all the pines had that bright color of new needles, the maples and birches were just throwing leaves, and even the blackberry bramble that rolled under the trees still looked fresh. Moss clung to the edges of rocks, looking vibrant and soft.

Sam took deep breathes as they rolled past the stop sign, breathing in the clear air. Even Al relaxed a fraction as they left the areas where humans were most populous.

Trees lined the road on either side of them, reaching up and cutting off the sky until it was a single, thin blue ribbon above. Sam knew that once she stopped, the sound of birdsong would fill in the gaps between the passing cars. Deer, bunnies, and even the occasional fox might pass by in the undergrowth. Elk also regularly made their way through the area, though the ones around here were bigger than her Jeep.

Just past the land preserved by the state as a watershed, they turned into a driveway at the bottom of a hill. The gate was shut and locked against the mundane humans who might try to gain access. It was also enspelled, something Sam had known before because she'd been told.

For the first time, she could *see* the spell dancing around the square box where someone had to type in the access code. The magic looked yellow and spiky, and smelled of oregano and mint.

"What would happen if you tried to use this keypad?" Sam asked as she put in her number.

The gate slowly, silently, swung inward.

Al glared at her. "Nothing," he said.

"It wouldn't zap you?" she said, curious. She put the Jeep back into gear and slid forward, pausing a few feet up, making sure the gate closed completely behind her.

"No, it wouldn't *zap* me," Al said, sounding exasperated. "It just wouldn't work."

"Because you're an elf?" Sam guessed.

"Because I'm not human," Al clarified. "Your grandmother was very set in her ways, and determined that only humans be allowed unmetered access to the estate."

Sam wasn't sure how to read the tone of his voice.

Was he pissed off? Hurt? He certainly didn't sound as though he approved of her grandmother's actions.

Then again, if he was a guardian for the portal, wouldn't he welcome the extra protection?

She shook her head. It was a detail that she'd have to see to later.

Woods branched out on either side of the long driveway. This wasn't a tame forest, where the trees had been planted carefully in rows. All manner of plants battled it out for dominance, growing thickly together. The blackberry bramble had also been allowed to grow, making it extremely difficult to pass through. Of course, there were a few animal trails, but even those weren't easy to find or pass along.

As they climbed the hill, Sam felt herself torn. On the one hand, she had so many (so many!) bad memories of this place. A part of her just wanted to turn around and drive back to her extremely cute condo located up on Capitol Hill.

Yet, at the same time, she felt a longing grow, a desire to be here, at the estate, on this land, that she'd never felt prior to now.

It was almost like coming home to a place she'd never truly seen before.

The road turned again as they neared the top of the quarter-mile long driveway. The trees grew closer in now. Sam had always felt this section of the woods, near the house, was more foreboding than the entranceway. She caught a whiff of mulch and dried leaves. A cool breeze made her shiver despite the wonderful heater in her vehicle.

Holly branches scratched the sides of the Jeep, as did the occasional red huckleberry leaning out too far over the driveway. Ocean spray also reared up and hung over, the white flowers just starting to blossom. The Indian plums had already ripened, and the fruit hung black against the yellow-green leaves. Bright yellow flowers topped the Oregon grape, buzzing with bees.

The estate had never felt so alive to Sam. Was it from the power she'd inherited? Or was it just the spring?

They finally pulled out of the darker part of the woods and into the clearing in front of the house.

Mansion, really. Big enough for twenty-plus people to gather together and sleep under a single roof for the holidays. Far too big for Grandma Starling on her own, particularly after Grandpa Starling had died, almost ten years ago.

However, Grandma Starling had been the keeper of the portal. She hadn't been about to leave. Fortunately, the portal and her magic kept her young. She'd still been going strong, even at ninety-two.

Sam grimaced as she pulled up and looked at the dark abode. She felt both of those urges again, the one prompting her to keep driving around the circular driveway and just leave, as well as the one that really, *really* wanted her to stay.

The mansion was primarily built out of solid wood from nearby fir trees, then stained a dark brown color. It had been constructed back in 1910, when the portal itself had been consecrated. A large, grand double door stood in the center of the front façade, with carved wooden pillars on either side of it, totally ridiculous given the rest of the more rustic-looking estate if you asked Sam. There had originally been a covered portico, shading guests getting into and out of their horse-drawn carriages. It had been taken out with the advent of cars, when a much wider space had been needed. Sam would have just widened the archway, because that shade would have been nice, and it also would have provided good cover during the inevitable rains.

The first floor of the mansion had eighteen-foot-tall ceilings, with long, skinny windows that matched, with wavy glass encased in wooden panes. They were a heat sink in the winter. Sam would have replaced them with something energy efficient ages ago. Plus, the many panes always looked like foreboding eyes glaring out at her, telling her to leave this place and never return.

The second story was less grand, though it had just as many old-fashioned windows. Only the attic was windowless, yet another dark place storing bad memories.

Sam sighed. Nothing would remove the gloom of this house. Not even a bright red paint, though painting over that wood would be a tragedy. Maybe just stripping it and putting a plain, glossy coat on it...Now that it was hers, perhaps she could do something with it.

She glanced over at her passenger.

Al appeared to be having similar unpleasant thoughts.

Then again, the portal was his duty, something he'd been assigned.

He was probably looking forward to dumping her

ass and getting back to his own plane, his own people. Hell, to return and restart his own life, if he'd been assigned here since Grandmother Starling had taken over, which had to be thirty years ago or more.

"Shall we?" Sam finally asked.

Before Al could reply, the front door opened and Sam's mother came out.

Rachael Dunham resembled Grandpa Starling, not Grandma. Her white-skinned face was triangular, with a broad forehead, flat cheeks, and a sharp chin. However, she took after both her parents in her disapproval of Sam and the stern look in eyes that were forever disapproving.

"What took you so long to get here?" Mom demanded as she swept down the stairs. She was in her usual "office chic" attire, though she hadn't worked a day in her life. The gray pencil skirt she wore would have looked better on a thirty-year-old, and her peach-colored blouse was too frilly. However, her shocking white and silver hair looked beautiful. Sam had always thought it was her mom's best feature.

"I drove out here as soon as I heard the news," Sam said as she got out of the car.

Mom stopped short, a look of utter shock on her face. "Heard the news? You didn't feel it?"

"You're right. I misspoke," Sam said, the apology far too familiar. "I felt Grandma Starling's passing first."

"Thank the Goddess," Mom said.

Sam nearly rolled her eyes. The portals were strictly non-denominational. Mom, however, had gotten in with a sect of witches who worshiped a Goddess Gaia creator type being, back when she'd been a teenager. She'd managed to convert Morgan's wife Laureen into the cult, though Sam wouldn't have anything to do with either of them.

"I'm sorry about Grandma Starling," Sam said. It had been her mother's mother who'd just passed.

For a moment, a brief flash of what Sam would have call humanity flashed over her mother's face. "Thank you," Mom said, her tone finally softening. "She hadn't been feeling well. We'd just checked her into the hospital yesterday. I hadn't expected her passing to be so sudden."

Sam nodded, a small sliver of guilt slicing through her. She hadn't been around, hadn't called, hadn't known that her grandmother wasn't well, or been admitted to the hospital.

Then again, no one in her family had thought to call her to tell her about it either.

"But you should have just used a portal to get here. Not driven," Mom added, tossing a glare in Al's direction for good measure.

"Then what would I have done with the Jeep?" Sam asked. "I couldn't have just left it in the parking lot at work."

Mom shook her head instead of continuing with the argument. "You need to come inside now. *We* all came by portal, and have been waiting for you."

With that, she turned and went back inside.

Sam sighed and trudged forward.

Al sprang in front of her, reaching for the oversized door of the mansion.

What, did he think she couldn't open her own door? She wasn't some frail, overly polite lady.

Before she could growl at him, Al turned to her, his golden eyes blazing with an odd light.

"You are the guardian of the portal. Only you," he told her fiercely. "No one else. Remember that."

Then he did hold the door open for Sam.

Sam straightened her shoulders and lifted her head up. It felt as though she'd just been given a pep talk before marching into battle.

Probably because any encounter with her family was sure to be a fight.

CHAPTER

SIX

ON THE FIRST FLOOR, the rooms of the mansion all connected to each other either through open archways or doors. It made it very easy to circle around the house, one room leading to the next.

The portal room sat in the very center of the building and was deliberately easy to overlook.

Sam didn't pay much attention to the rooms she passed through. They were as dark and dismal as she remembered. It was as if no sunlight were ever allowed to enter those tall windows never opened for spring breezes.

So she went through the front greeting room, the stiffly formal dining room (though it did have beautiful built-in sideboards), one of the three studies, then turned the corner, going up the back hallway.

Midway down the hallway stood two doors. The one on her right led to a small mud room/porch that no one ever used: the family always went out to the backyard through the kitchen.

The other door, to her left, was plain. It had that '70s air about it, flat and cheap. It looked as though it led to a broom closet or perhaps the basement. The only thing that gave it away was the vivid golden glow of wards that danced around the frame, wards that Sam had only vaguely noticed before but that now shown brighter than any neon beer sign.

The brass door handle tingled against Sam's palm as she turned it. This door was also enspelled, and even fewer could enter unaccompanied.

Sam pushed the door open, held it for her companion, then closed it firmly behind him.

The first thing she noticed was the portal.

Hell, the *only* thing she could see at first was the portal. The rest of the room faded into darkness.

The portal itself rose all the way up to that tall, eighteen-foot ceiling. The front pillars, each about two feet around, were fluted. They'd been carved out of a golden wood that resembled burly oak, but Sam knew that the wood came from a tree not grown on the earthly plane. A gracefully curved piece made up an arch that brushed the ceiling, connecting the front pillars and setting them about twelve feet apart. The arch was constructed from a different, darker wood, more red in color and also not from around here.

The rear two pillars weren't as impressive. They stood about eight feet back from the front pair, though the same twelve feet apart from each other. Sam had always wondered if they'd been added at a different time. They were just as tall, but again, made from a different wood, one that held onto its green, immature look. Instead of fluted columns, they were plain, with ornately carved crowns and feet. The same reddish wood connected the pair of them at the top, as well as to the front pillars.

Sam had always thought of the portal room as dark and dank, like a wet basement. The air still felt cool to her, but refreshingly so. She didn't smell mold, but magic, like tomato-basil soup with just a hint of cayenne underneath, warm and homey, the perfect thing on a cold, rainy day. In addition, she noticed an underlying scent, something exotic and otherworldly, like a taste of something she'd never had but still remembered.

In between the four pillars swirled a black mist, like a mysterious, unknowable cube. Sam wasn't sure if the pillars contained the mist, holding it back, or if the mist was strung out between them, like a solid spiderweb.

For the first time, Sam saw sparks of light in the dark mist. Finger-length beams of purple danced between the clouds, along with golden splotches that would appear and disappear, like fireflies.

"About time you showed up," came a nasally voice to the side.

Sam shook her head. The allure of the portal faded to something she could more easily ignore, though now that she'd felt it, seen it with new eyes, she knew the portal would be a marker for her.

She'd never be lost, not anywhere in the whole wide world of the earthly plane. She'd always know exactly where home was, now.

At least, geographically.

There were others in the portal room. Her mother, of

course. Her father stood there as well. He was also a witch, with some power, though not as much as her mom. While her mom had always had everything to say when it came to Sam and how she was failing the family, her father had never said anything at all. She was surprised he was even here.

Maybe he'd come due to some misguided belief that his wife was actually going to grieve the loss of her mother.

Aunt Karen, her mother's sister, was also there, along with her two sons, Brady and Vernon. Aunt Karen looked enough like her mom that they could have been twins, right down to the disapproving look they were currently giving her.

Sam had never been close to these cousins. She'd frequently referred to them as "Tweedledumb and Tweedledumber." They looked like the kind of bodyguards that loan sharks used, wearing dark suits that barely fit their muscled shoulders and broad bellies, their hair lanky, their expressions equally slack, just waiting for the command to go fetch something. Or break someone's leg.

Morgan was also there. He stood beside the portal. A small end table had been dragged into the room.

Now that Sam was thinking about it, the portal room was suspiciously bare.

Where was Grandma Starling's big wingback chair? Sam remembered her sitting on it like a throne, receiving visitors. And there were other things missing as well—an ugly blue-green couch, and a torchier lamp.

A whirring noise refocused her attention back

toward Morgan. A strange mechanism sat on the table in front of him, a device that appeared to be made out of brass, with several interlocking wheels already spinning. The top of it was like a windmill, though with the spiky blades parallel to the floor. It gave off a lecherous purple glow.

Morgan had been the one with the nasally voice. He wore collegiate looking clothes, with a tweed jacket, complete with leather patches on the elbows, an off-white turtleneck, and black pants. Really, the only thing missing was a carved meerschaum pipe.

"Sam decided to drive here," her mother said scornfully. "But now that she's finally shown up, we can get down to business."

"Which is?" Sam said. She didn't like the sound of that, or the way that all of her supposed family was now looking at her, as though she was a particularly tasty leg of lamb that Grandma Starling had just put on the table.

"You obviously have no idea how to work the portal," her mother continued. "So we are here to help you."

"Help me? How?" Sam asked, though she really wanted to throw it into her mother's face that it wasn't her fault that no one had bothered teaching her anything.

No, her older brother had been the golden child. She'd been the left-over, the "heir and the spare" as it were.

Except that she hadn't even been granted that. Once her parents had discovered just how pervasive her dyslexia was, they'd given up on her.

"Until you go through your training period, we want

Morgan to be co-steward of the portal," Aunt Karen said, stepping into the breach.

At least she'd bothered changing into some sort of mourning clothes, wearing a shapely black dress, her good pearls, and heels that Sam would have broken her neck trying to walk in.

"My training period?" Sam asked, glancing at Al. He stood just to the side of her, hands behind his back, still looking like a fancy lawyer, albeit one starring in a billion-dollar fantasy movie, given the filigree webbing of his ears and the slight glow to his golden eyes.

He nodded. "Generally a year or so, while you and the portal become attuned to one another. And while the magical power you've inherited becomes adapted to its new host, so it isn't as easily stolen."

"And what happens after a year?" Sam said, still dubious. She hadn't forgotten Al's warning either, that she was the sole guardian of the portal.

Would Morgan, once he'd gotten a taste of that power, merely step aside? Or would he arrange for some sort of accident to happen to her?

Was that what had happened to Grandma Starling? Had her brother organized something bad to befall her? If so, no wonder the portal chose someone else. It was self-defense, one of the rules about portals that Sam had actually been taught. The killer of a portal guardian *never* received the portal's power.

"Morgan will step aside after a year, of course," Mom assured Sam.

The smirk on Morgan's face said otherwise, though

he smoothed it away so quickly Sam wondered if she'd just been projecting.

"And what if I don't want a co-guardian? If I think that I can handle the portal myself?" Sam said, feeling her back starting to straighten, her gut pull in, her stomach settle.

Just one of the many fights she and her family were committed to.

"I'm afraid we're not going to give you much choice in that," Mom said.

Sam hadn't noticed Tweedledumb and Tweedledumber placing themselves behind her.

"No!" she cried when they grabbed hold of her. She started struggling immediately. She wasn't some easy lamb to be led to the slaughter. She pushed her feet back, but they were much stronger than she was.

"No!" she screamed, throwing a glance at Al.

"You cannot," her mother intoned, pointing a finger at the elf. "It is up to the humans how they handle the human side of the portal. The non-humans have no say, as long as we aren't damaging the portal. And you know that."

Al maintained an impressive veneer of calm, though Sam suspected that he was frustrated. The way his nostrils flared was also probably an indication of anger.

"The gate guardian has stated that she doesn't want this," Al said, taking a step forward.

A warning light sprang from her mother's finger. It didn't quite zap the elf, falling a good foot in front of him. Sam heard the sizzle as she continued her struggles, trying to free her arms from the meaty paws that held her as tight as iron. At least they'd stopped dragging her forward, waiting for the conversation to finish.

"The gate guardian is uneducated and has no idea what she's doing," her mom said sternly. "If she were five years old, your people wouldn't say a word, even if she were struggling and objecting in a similar manner."

Al pressed his lips together tighter and looked to the side, before taking a step back. "I still plan on bringing up this highly unorthodox behavior to the council."

Great. There went her only chance of being saved.

Looked like Sam was going to have to do it herself.

Tweedledumb and Tweedledumber started dragging her inexorably forward again, toward Morgan's malevolent machine. She'd never seen such a thing before, hadn't ever heard of it. There weren't that many enchanted items that she was aware of. They took too much magic both to manufacture as well as maintain.

The purple light surrounding it began to coalesce into a solid figure—a grasping hand, reaching out toward her.

She couldn't let it touch her. It would strip her of all her power, not merely take some so she would share it with Morgan. She knew that. She suspected her mother might as well.

Had he created a warlock machine? So he, himself, wouldn't be considered a warlock, but still a witch?

It was the kind of hair-splitting of the rules that her family occasionally engaged in.

A bright flickering to her right momentarily drew her attention.

The portal.

The purple lights floating in the mist had grown agitated, at least as far as Sam could tell. Instead of being finger sized, they were now puffed up and spiky, like a moss and lichen covered fat twig. The edges of each one vibrated with energy.

Sam wasn't sure how she knew to reach out her hand toward them. Some of that training she'd never received must have been passed along with Grandma Starling's power.

The purple lights leaped from the mist, striking her palm with tingling, sharp blows, like stinging rain.

Sam absorbed the power being granted to her as greedily as Morgan's machine might have done.

The magic sank deep into her core, soaking her in a cool, brine-smelling spray. It pooled there for a moment, gathering up strength, before hurling itself outward, infusing her skin and then flowing outward.

A current of raw energy came alive under Tweedledumb and Tweedledumber's hands. Not only did they let her go, but the power she threw at them knocked the pair of them on their asses as least five feet away from her.

Sam turned to face her mother.

"**I said no**," she intoned.

The words echoed strangely in her head, as if she'd been granted a microphone with the perfect amount of reverb.

"But—" her mother started.

"**No. Get out. Now**," Sam said, her voice still sounding monstrously loud in her ears.

She pointed a finger at Morgan's machine, the ugly

purple claw still reaching out and grasping. A golden streak of lightning leaped out from her, smashing into the gears. The machine blew itself to pieces.

Feeling smugly pleased when the shrapnel cut into Morgan's clothes might have been a little petty. Maybe. A smidge.

There was a moment of silence as Sam's mother, father, brother, and aunt all exchanged looks.

Finally, her mother nodded. "Fine," she said. "You appear to have some affinity for magic after all." She speared Sam with a sharp gaze. "We will talk about this later."

Sam didn't bother saying anything until her mother had swept out of the room. Then she muttered, just to herself, "Maybe when hell actually freezes over."

Her aunt, cousins, and brother all slunk away.

When her father reached the door, he turned back and glanced at her, then gave her an unexpected thumbs up before he also slipped out the door.

That...wasn't helpful, actually.

Did he actually approve of Sam?

Then why the hell hadn't he ever said anything to stop his wife?

That thumbs up might have made things worse in Sam's opinion of her family.

She couldn't say how she knew they were leaving. But one by one, she felt them flit away, their footsteps no longer weighing on her consciousness. They all took portals they'd previously prepared, going wherever they'd be going.

Could she follow them? If she'd wanted to?

Grandma Starling had had that ability. Maybe she'd learn it too, someday.

Sam drew out a deep breath as she turned to face Al.

The elf gave her a tight smile.

"Well done," he said, the words coming out in his normal, snooty tone. "Now, you're going to have to learn as much as you can about the portal and its magic. And soon."

Why did that sound more like a threat than anything else?

CHAPTER
SEVEN

As Sam and Al left the portal room, she turned back and ran her fingers over the wards. The last of the purple, spiky power that had been granted her by the portal seeped away, flowing into the wards as well as back into the room.

The protections around the door would be much stronger, now. She didn't think she could actually block her family from entering the portal room—at least, not yet.

Sam felt drained, both emotionally and physically as she led Al to the big kitchen in the back corner of the mansion. It was, in her opinion, the homiest room in the entire place.

Not that it was comfortable. Not by a long shot. It had all stainless steel, professional-grade appliances, a huge farmhouse style sink, and enough counter space for a catering crew of six to all be preparing food at the same time

However, on one side stood a wooden breakfast bar,

with tall wooden stools. The windows back here were more modern, and had probably been opened sometime in the last decade. This area always smelled of Grandma Starling's good coffee. The whole kitchen tended to be warmer as well than the rest of the house—heating those eighteen foot ceilings took some doing.

Sam turned to Al. "I'm starving," she said. It was only about four in the afternoon, but it seemed as though lunch had been several days ago.

She turned around in the kitchen, then turned around again. She didn't want to have to go out somewhere to get takeout. Delivery meant going down and waiting by the gate for the person with the food to arrive.

"It's now your house," Al said gently.

"I know. It just feels weird going through Grandma's fridge," Sam complained.

Al merely shrugged. "Wouldn't she want you to? Rather than see good food go to waste?"

Sam had to nod at that. Yes, that was exactly what Grandma Sterling would say.

Luckily, there appeared to be leftovers in the fridge that should be eaten now, though some were past their prime and needed to be tossed out. Sam recognized the name of a nearby Italian restaurant on one of the boxes of take away, and to her delight discovered half of a left-over ribeye, in a beautiful brown butter and caper sauce.

Al shook his head. "Really?" he said. "You're going to eat that?"

"What, I suppose you exist only on twigs and leaves," Sam replied.

"You do not have to take a life to maintain your life," Al said primly.

"You do if you want any flavor or taste," Sam said. She found a pasta salad that didn't appear to have any meat or seafood in it for Al.

They sat on either side of the breakfast bar with their respective meals. Sam was in heaven with the ribeye. It had been perfectly cooked, warmed up well in the microwave, and the sauce was divine. She drank two large glasses of water with it, wondering if the magic had left her dehydrated. That was something she'd have to be aware of.

She purposefully sat looking out of the window, with her back to the rest of the house. She knew she'd feel it if someone was near, or tried to enter the building.

There wasn't much to see behind the house. There was a large yard covered in manicured grass, edged with rows of wild roses. They vied with the blackberry bramble in terms of fierce thorns. Past the rose barrier was all trees. The property extended for several acres in all directions. A nature preserve butted up against the entire northern side of it. The southern side, to the "corner" where the road turned, was hers. Back behind the property were railroad tracks, and the railroad owned a large swath of land on either side of it. Together, this meant that there were no neighbors for miles.

Sam breathed in the quiet. She'd always considered herself a city girl. Too much quiet left her antsy. She suspected that just hearing natural sounds would get to her now and again, that she would miss the sounds of traffic and the city, but right then, it was nice.

Al looked out on the kitchen, watching her back, as it were.

The meal wasn't much, but it was enough. Sam stretched when she finished, taking the dishes over to the sink and washing them up, leaving them in the drying rack before she turned back to Al.

"So, now what?" she asked.

"Time to start learning," Al said.

Again, why did that sound so much like a threat?

Sam sighed, but nodded. It made sense. Though learning had always been full of pits, snares, and traps for her.

She followed Al back to the portal room, then opened the door and followed him in. The portal still called to her, inviting her to stare at it for hours, commune with it, share all her thoughts.

Again she warned herself to not go in too deep.

With a determined shake of her head, Sam looked away from the portal and watched as Al made his way over to the wall to the right of the door, past the ever tempting portal.

"Should I go and get a torchier?" she asked as he started perusing the bookshelves that she hadn't ever paid attention to before.

He glanced back at her. "No, I can see in the dark," he said. He sounded as haughty as ever, particularly as he added, "You could bring the lights up in the room."

"What do you mean?" Sam asked. "Is there a light switch in here somewhere?"

Al sighed. She'd give him a high rank on the emo scale for that one.

"*You* are the 'light switch,' as it were," he said plainly. "You can control the room. The entire manor, for that matter. Even the surrounding landscape, to some extent."

"Wait, so it doesn't always have to be dark and gloomy in here?" Sam said, surprised.

"Your grandmother often mistook *dark* for *serious*," Al said. He sounded as disapproving as always.

"Huh," Sam said. Thinking back, she did remember that Grandma Starling was almost always dressed in black. She also dressed formally. Not in dresses, but full pants and occasionally long skirts. Never a T-shirt and jeans.

Sam wasn't sure how to turn up the lights in the room. She could feel Al's eyes on her as she held out her arms, hands up, then lifted them, imagining she was raising the lights with them.

Nothing.

That wasn't how lights worked. Sam *knew* how lights worked. She'd pulled enough electrical wire through walls to understand how to set up a light switch, or connect up a breaker.

According to her mother, her lack of magic was partially a failure of imagination. Sam always needed to see things, touch them, in order to replicate them. She wasn't good at coming up with something new on the fly. Hell, even the lightning bolt she'd issued earlier at Morgan's machine had been inspired by the insipid flare that her mother had sent towards Al.

Sam determinedly walked back toward the door of the portal room. There, to the left of the door as it opened. That was where she'd put a light switch.

What kind of light would she put in here? She turned and looked back at the rest of the room.

The high ceilings were key. There was a picture rail set into the walls maybe a foot down from the ceiling. If Sam was remodeling this room, she'd put in track lighting—a line of halogen lights on top of that picture rail, aiming each light up, toward the ceiling. That would produce a nice, bright light without any of it shining in her eyes. She'd put the lights on a dimmer switch as well, so she could perfectly adjust the brightness to her mood.

After Sam had everything pictured firmly in mind, only then did she turn around and face the room, her back to the door. She closed her eyes and reached out, her fingers brushing against the wall where she'd install the outlet box for a single light switch.

When she opened her eyes again, the room was lit up perfectly. It was exactly as she'd imagined it, with the lights all shining upward, illuminating the white ceiling. It was curved along the edges, something she hadn't realized before. Cool.

Now, Sam could get a proper look at the room.

It was roughly twenty by twenty, with the portal standing in the center of it.

Bookshelves lined the walls to the right and left of the portal. She hadn't realized that there were so many books in here. Of course, that immediately made her feel claustrophobic.

So many words she couldn't read.

The bookshelves were made from golden-oak tiger wood, the spots and lines enhancing their beauty, with carved molding along the tops and sides, a pattern of intertwined vines. Leaded glass done in diamond shapes covered the top shelves that were a good seven feet up. The doors protecting the bottom shelves were just plain glass. Given the quality of the construction, she'd bet that the bookshelves were either original to the mansion or installed shortly after construction had been completed.

Al was perusing the bookshelf to her right, and already had a few large, leather covered tomes in his hands. They were sure to be dusty, though she didn't smell any of that nose-tickling old book smell. She wouldn't be able to read a word of them, she just knew it.

The bookshelf on her left had different books. Sam couldn't say why they struck her as odd. Maybe the books there weren't in English, or any human tongue. They weren't as uniform as the books on the shelves to the right. Several of the spines were also colorful.

Though chances were that she could hardly read a single word of those books either, at least they looked less daunting.

Directly behind the portal stood a large white fireplace. The mantle took up much of the wall. A huge carving that Sam had never taken a good look at hung above the mantle shelf. The actual fireplace itself was gas, the wood-burning version replaced in the 1970s, she'd guess. She walked around the portal, ignoring how much she wanted to stare into it, lose herself in its gently swirling mists, and walked to the mantle.

It surprised her to see how many pictures Grandma Starling had perched on the mantle: pictures of her mother as a young girl, pictures of Aunt Karen, pictures of Grandpa Starling, as well as pictures of all the cousins. There was even one of Sam herself, a picture taken without her knowing about it, probably at one of the family get-togethers. She was seated at one of the formal dining room tables, laughing at something.

Why were these pictures here? Grandma Starling didn't have anything else like them, anywhere in the mansion.

Yet, here they were. And this was the heart of the home, at least for a portal keeper.

It showed a side of Grandma Starling that she hadn't shown to her family, or at least not to Sam.

How long had these pictures been here? Had they always resided in this room, hidden away from the casual visitors to the mansion? Only visible to those coming through the portal?

Were these Grandma Starling's true feelings showing?

Sam regretted once again that she hadn't spent more time with her grandmother, who had occasionally been slightly more decent to her than her own parents.

Not a high bar.

Sam took a step back and looked up at the carving above the fireplace mantle. It was oval in shape, sticking out from the wall by a good six inches. Like the mantle, it had been painted white. Similar to the bookshelves, a thick braided carving of vines encircled the oval.

Now that Sam was closer, she could see that many smaller ovals had been carved into the concave face of the main one. The longer she peered at it, the more details she could make out.

Each of the smaller ovals wasn't quite flat white. No, they had a touch of shimmer to them. Perhaps even opalescence, in the right lights.

And they weren't stationary. They floated very slowly in the space, traversing and nearly touching one another before drifting away. New ones came up from behind then disappeared again.

"It isn't an accurate representation of all the worlds that the Choowe portal connects to," Al said as he came up to stand beside Sam. "It's merely representational."

"A lot of worlds, floating around?" Sam asked as she looked more closely.

"I believe that was the intent," Al said, still disapproving. "You humans are always trying to make art that can be used instead of a proper portal. Like those tapestries in France."

Sam had no idea what he was talking about, but before she could ask, he shoved a large pile of books at her.

"Here," Al said. "These should give you a good start."

She reached out and grasped the pile. There were at least half a dozen books there, each more solemn than the next.

She looked at the pile in her hands, then turned and

headed for the door, skirting the siren call of the portal. Al opened the door for her—she was surprised that he could do that, open the door from the inside and not from the outside—and she followed him back into the kitchen.

With a loud thud, Sam placed the large pile of books on the table, then slowly pulled the first one off the pile.

The cover of the book was made from a faded, gray leather. Golden text was embossed on the front of it, along with what looked like several arches underneath it.

It took her a few tries to spell out the title—*A Compendium of Working Portals.*

Sounded truly soporific.

Sam slowly opened the book to the first page of text.

Instead of being typed words, it was all hand-written, in cursive.

To her eyes, it was as if someone had drawn a line across the page, with some loops above and below the center of it. That was it. She couldn't even make out a single word.

She closed the book and glared at Al. "Is there an audio version?" she asked, trying to make light of the situation. "Maybe a YouTube channel?"

Al blinked, surprised. "I would think that you'd want to learn all you could about the portals. To protect both the Choowe portal as well as yourself." He pointed to a book further down in the pile. "I included a bestiary, as it were, to help you familiarize yourself with the denizens of the more common netherworlds, so you might have a better chance of fighting and beating the next one you encounter."

Sam sighed. "I do want to learn. Truly. I just...I can't read."

"What do you mean, you can't read?" Al asked, horrified. "Everyone can read."

Sam gave him a tight smile. "We're not going to get into the politics of literacy, at least not now," she said. "But there's a reason why my family didn't bother trying to teach me anything about magic or the portals. I have severe dyslexia."

At Al's puzzled look, she went on. "I have difficulty reading. The letters...dance and reverse themselves. They get all jumbled together. Printed pages, I can get some of what's there. But I miss a lot. And it takes a lot of effort and time for me to put the words together."

"You did graduate from one of those institutes of supposed higher learning on this plane, didn't you?" Al demanded.

"No, I didn't." Sam shook her head. "I made my way through high school by the skin of my teeth. That was all the 'learning' I could take. And the only reason I passed was because of Tami, my best friend. She read all the assignments to me out loud."

Tami now lived in Bellevue, happily married with a three-year-old and a second on the way. They still got together every other month or so, giving Tami a night off from the family, just to see "the girls" as it were.

Al still looked horrified.

"I'm kind of being serious when I ask if there's an audio version of these available," Sam said, pointing toward the books. "Otherwise, it'll take me months to read through them. And I don't know how much I'll retain."

Al looked away for a moment. He had that tell again, of pressing his lips together, holding in what he wanted to say.

"What is it?" Sam finally prompted.

Al sighed, deflating. "I don't know why the portal chose you," he admitted softly. "Particularly since you can't read."

Sam bristled. Just because she couldn't read well or easily didn't mean she was uneducated, some country bumpkin.

Before Sam could round off on Al, he said softly, without looking at her, "If anyone asks, I did *not* teach this to you. It was something you discovered on your own."

Surprised, Sam nodded.

Al opened the book with the handwritten pages, then he took one of her rough hands in one of his smooth, cool ones. He chanted something in a foreign language (Elvish?) as he dragged her finger across the first line, then the second, then the third.

Sam felt the magic rolling off Al. It smelled of cinnamon and pine. Then a wet cloud sank into the bare skin of the back of her hand as the magic flowed into her.

Suddenly, a very properly British voice piped up, saying, "There are many working portals, all over the world. In addition, there are many types of portals.

What exactly does this author mean by a working portal? We—"

The voice suddenly cut off as Sam lifted her finger from the page and Al withdrew his hand. "Wait a minute," she said. "I can get these books to read themselves to me?"

Al nodded. "It's just something you picked up," he said evasively.

Sam paused, considering. The spell hadn't taken much power. Books *wanted* to share their information.

Al showed her the spell a couple more times.

First, Sam reached for the shape of the spell, trying to reconfigure it in her head.

All spells had a shape that needed to be focused on, an outline of the form that the witch then filled with magic.

This one was, unsurprisingly, in the vague shape of a pointed finger, though the hand attached to it seemed to have an additional five fingers, not four. Then she had to get the scent right, not of moldering books (which was honestly what she'd expected for her version of the spell). The cinnamon and pine.

She knew that human and elf versions of a spell were likely to be different, as they'd be associated with different things. The human version retained the scent of fresh pine, probably for the paper, but for her, the spell then added the chemical odor of ink, which she related to furniture dye.

Finally, Sam put all the pieces together and was able to run the spell herself.

The book picked up right where she'd ended, talking about how the author had decided to define *working portal* as a portal that had a permanent location and was connected to the netherworlds, not the temporary portals witches created to travel across a single plane of existence.

So the book wasn't going to be a complete snooze, though the author talking about himself in the third person was already annoying.

"Can I get any book to do that?" Sam demanded, lifting her finger from the page again. The only way she'd ever been able to enjoy reading was through audiobooks. She'd discovered those in the last few years. They'd made the commute to the woodworking shop so much more pleasant.

"Yes," Al said. "But you have to focus on the magic."

"So I have to be touching the page?" Sam said.

"Of course," Al said, dismissively.

Too bad. Though maybe once she got some practice, she could get the book to just read itself to her while she was driving, or doing the dishes, or even working.

"All right," Sam said. She turned back to the book, but her anger wouldn't let her continue. "Does everyone know this spell? To make a book read itself out loud?" As she'd picked it up fairly easily, and it took so little magic, it seemed as though it might be a common spell.

"I believe so," Al said. He paused, staring hard at her. "What's wrong?"

"Why the *hell* didn't anyone teach me that spell earlier?" Sam said as the rage built. "Why did my family just decide to abandon me, letting me pick up what few scraps of magic I could, instead of giving me a way to learn?"

Al opened his mouth then shut it again. He took a deep breath, then replied in an overly calm manner, as if talking to a complete psychotic who needed to be calmed down before she went nuclear.

All right, so perhaps he wasn't completely wrong in his approach.

"Magic isn't generally taught this way," he said slowly. "Normally, a witch *has* to be able to read about a spell and then determine how to do it herself. For all that witches might be considered outside of the norm here on this plane, they are incredibly conservative. Preserving tradition has meant survival."

"To the point that they'll kick out one of their own?" Sam demanded.

"Yes," Al said. "A century ago, they might have just killed you, or sent you to an orphanage instead of trying to raise you," he added pitilessly. "Despite whatever magic you may have had."

That didn't make Sam's current situation any better. Nor her mood.

"Fine," she said. "So we're a fucking ruthless lot. Go us." She shook her head in disgust.

She already had so many problems with her birth family. Hating them more wasn't going to help anyone.

Particularly now that she was going to have to deal with them on a regular basis again.

"I need to get out of here," Sam said, looking around the foreign kitchen, the unfamiliar quiet abruptly pressing in on her.

"But this is your home, now," Al complained.

Really, how did he manage to sneer and whine so much in a single sentence?

"I can't stay here. Not tonight," Sam said before he could object again. "I need to go home. To my home."

"You aren't safe there," Al said sternly, scolding her as if she were five.

"Then come along with me," Sam said. She grabbed the pile of books and started walking toward the front door.

"Wait, where are you going?" Al asked. He actually reached out and grabbed her arm, as if he was going to stop her.

Sam did stop, but only to warn him. "Let go of me, or I'll make you let go of me," she growled.

Al released her immediately and took a step back, his hands up. "I apologize for touching you unasked. That was incredibly rude of me."

"Just make sure it doesn't happen again," Sam said. However, he'd cut off her momentum. "I was going to get my Jeep and drive home."

"Why don't you just open a portal?" Al asked. "Then, you can come back here in the morning, refreshed, and pick up your vehicle."

That…actually made sense. Sam was usually a good driver, but given the shocks of the day and how exhausted she felt, perhaps driving wasn't the best idea in the world. Plus, it would take over an hour to get back to her condo, probably longer given rush hour traffic.

"All right," Sam said. She walked slowly back to the kitchen, depositing the books back on the breakfast bar.

At least creating a portal was something her parents *had* taught her.

The easiest type of portal to build had two ends. A single, one-way portal was much more difficult to construct, and almost impossible to maintain. A portal needed a solid anchor. Creating a two-way tunnel, but treating it as a one-way, left the witch drained for an inexplicable amount of time. Even after the portal was released, it was as if it continued to tap into the witch's power.

Sam used a finger and a marker spell to create this end of the portal. She held the shape of an abstract character in her head. She'd been told it was based on the Chinese ideogram for *home*.

The marker held this end of the portal open. Even in her exhausted state, Sam found that creating the portal marker was easier than ever, probably due to the influx of Grandma Sterling's magic.

The scents she remembered were of orange blossoms and licorice, a strange combination but it made sense in her head. Though it didn't remind her of her home, it at least was very memorable.

Then she flung the portal outward. That was how she'd always envisioned it, a sweeping motion of her hand with a flick of the wrist at the end, like unfurling a rug or a towel.

The other end of the portal landed squarely in the living room of her condo. Never before had she had such a clear impression of exactly where a portal stuck.

Generally speaking, even if she was creating a portal to her condo, a place she was incredibly familiar with, it still might take her two or three tries to get the opening to land where she wanted it.

The extra power she'd inherited from Grandma Starling continued to make her life better in some ways, that was for damned sure.

She picked up her reading assignment for the evening, then paused for a moment, double checking with Al.

"Coming?" she asked.

He sighed, ranking pretty high on the emo scale. "I guess so."

"I'll even get the blow up bed for you to use," Sam told him, as she didn't have a couch that he could sleep on.

"Gee. Thanks," Al said, grimacing.

Sam shrugged. There was only so much she could do for an unexpected guest.

All she wanted right now, though, was to go home.

CHAPTER

EIGHT

SAM STEPPED out of the cool embrace of the portal into the living room of her condo.

Home sweet home.

Al stepped out immediately behind her. He seemed upset. "I should have gone first," he said as he looked around. "In case something was here to attack you."

"Naw, we're safe here," Sam told him. She walked over to the coffee table in front of the big, over-stuffed chair in the corner and dumped the books down on it. "Can I get you anything? Coffee? Tea? I think I still have some chocolate chip ice cream."

After verifying that they were, indeed, alone, Al walked from the center of the room over to the book-shelves between the windows. "Did you build these?" he asked, running a finger along the smooth, blond oak.

"I did," Sam said with pride.

She'd pretty much gutted the condo when she'd bought it. It had needed it. It was partly why she'd been able to afford it. The little old lady who'd owned it before her hadn't done any work to it in decades.

The building had been constructed back in 1913. All of the units had originally been created with built-in Murphy beds in the living room. One of the first things Sam had done was tear out the cheap paneling that someone had used to enclose the space where the bed had been and put up proper sheetrock, making a usable closet. On the far end of it, she'd put in a stacked washer and dryer.

The floors were still the original Douglas fir. The little old lady had kept rugs covering everything so the wood was actually in pretty good shape. Most of the work Sam had put into the unit had been upgrading the knob-and-tube wiring, modernizing the bathroom (though keeping the original, claw-foot tub), as well as completely revamping the kitchen. She'd left the bedroom pretty much intact, merely replacing the rickety accordion doors of the closet and putting in a ceiling fan.

After that, it had been a series of small, slow improvements. She'd built three bookcases for the living room, one on either side of the two large windows on the far wall and one in between them. She'd filled the shelves not with books but with the various art projects that she was particularly pleased with. LED light strips attached to the bottom of each shelf illuminated the spaces.

The far left case held pots and bowls from when she'd been doing a lot of pottery. Many of the pieces were glazed in a beautiful blue-green color that she'd never been able to replicate.

Then she'd started doing fused glass, and had a whole set of standing glass plates that were both delicate and lovely, the colors melting into each other. The glass pieces were in the center case, along with some photographs she'd taken while hiking.

Most recently, Sam had gotten into poured acrylic paints. There were only a couple of canvases that she really liked and had put on her shelves so far, to the right.

"These are lovely," Al said, looking at her work then looking back at her. "I had no idea."

"What, were you expecting some sort of hovel?" Sam asked.

"Something like that, yes," Al said. His sly grin told her he was teasing. "Your work is a bit rustic. It would never grace an elven hall. But it's still very beautiful."

"Thanks, I think," Sam said. "Want some ice cream?"

"It doesn't have meat in it, does it?" Al asked, suspicious.

Sam rolled her eyes at him. "No, it's all vegetarian. It isn't vegan, though."

Al gave a disapproving sniff, but still said, "All right. That will have to do."

Sam went into her kitchen. It was a one-butt kitchen, barely big enough for her, even though she'd taken out the wall separating the original kitchen from the living room. The tall cupboards were from the 1970s, made from cheap wood. She'd painted them a beautiful bronze color that matched the new tiles she'd put on the floor. Eventually, she'd get around to replacing them.

The counters had been rotting when she'd bought the place, so she'd rebuilt them herself, having Juan come over one weekend to help hold things in place. She'd started with a cheap countertop and had only recently replaced it with a much higher grade marble one. As part of the remodel, she'd put in an under-the-counter, two drawer refrigerator/freezer. It had been one of the best purchases she'd made, leaving her space for a bigger stove on the other side.

Not as if she cooked that much, but it was still nice to have the option to bake a full-sized roast and have leftovers for a week rather than having to deal with a skinny, two ring stovetop and oven.

Sam scooped out two generous portions of ice cream into plain bowls, heated up a smaller bowl of fudge to pour over them, and brought that all out to the living room. She handed one bowl to Al, who was still looking at her artwork, before she sank into her chair.

As soon as she stopped moving, Sam realized just how tired she was. Damn. She'd planned on getting through at least half of the first book tonight, but she wasn't sure she had enough energy.

She knew there was a spell for drawing power from the nether planes, that a witch could use to bolster themselves, but it was tricky, and right on the edge of her previously limited abilities. Beyond that, it could be addictive, as well as dangerous. Once the spell ran its course, the original exhaustion would slam down like a pallet full of concrete blocks.

The danger came in making sure that the link to the netherworlds was completely severed afterward. Just ending that particular spell didn't guarantee that.

An open end could be sensed by whatever beings were in that netherworld. Theoretically, one could even hitch a ride to the earthly plane that way.

For now, Sam was just going to have to figure out her own way of muddling through, only using what she had.

Fortunately, she excelled at that sort of thing.

Al eventually finished perusing her shelves and sat down in the guest chair beside her.

"Why so many different forms of art?" he asked after he'd helped himself to a generous dollop of hot fudge on his ice cream.

Sam shrugged. "Got bored," she said honestly. "It's so exciting learning a new skill, mastering a new craft. Eventually, I'd find myself making the same thing over and over again, and it was time to move on."

Al shook his head. "You could have gone deeper into any of those crafts. Become a true master of it."

Sam snorted. "You sound like my mother," she said without rancor, just noting the fact. "No, I just never found anything that I wanted to study that much."

"Except the woodworking," Al said after a moment.

"Yeah, except that. But I do that for a living, so I wasn't about to just do that at night and on weekends as well," Sam pointed out. "Well, not all the time."

"You won't have to do it for a living anymore," Al said. "There is a very large inheritance waiting for you, as I understand it."

"Huh," Sam said. She hadn't really thought about it. Of course, there would be money. Grandma Starling hadn't ever worked. She didn't think Grandpa Starling had ever had a job, either.

She shook her head. It was hard to fathom that she, a proud union member, was now going to be part of the one percent. She couldn't imagine not going into the shop, seeing Juan and Pedro and the others every day.

Then again, her life had always been a bit different than the mundanes around her.

Now, it was just going to get pretty fucking weird.

"So, beyond guarding me, what do you do?" Sam asked.

Al considered for a moment, then put his empty ice cream dish down on the table.

"I don't necessarily protect you," Al said. "I protect what you represent, the power of the portal. It is the portal that I'm dedicated to."

Sam thought about that for a moment. Al wasn't invested in her, not personally. He was only concerned about the portal. She was going to have to remember that. Even if it did sting a bit.

Then again, she didn't really know much about the elves.

"You said you were assigned by the high council," Sam said. "Once your duty is over, what will you do?"

Al gave her a tight smile. "Return back to my home. Start my campaign to become a council member. Retake possession of my lands, which my brother is currently overseeing, in addition to his own lands."

"Get married? Have kids?" Sam asked.

Al shrugged. "In due course," he said. "There isn't anyone waiting for me, if that's what you're asking. I never became involved with anyone, as I knew where my duty lay."

"Which was protecting the portal?" Sam guessed.

"No, protecting the *human* side of the portal. There are other guardians for the Choowe portal, on the elven side, who guard that," he said.

"More than one?"

"Yes," Al said. "It's much more important to keep the door locked from our side, as it were."

"You don't trust humans very much, do you?" Sam said.

"Would you?"

All Sam could do was nod in response.

No, she wouldn't trust her people either.

CHAPTER
NINE

SAM ONLY GOT through a few chapters of the compendium about portals before she found she could no longer retain any of the information coming at her. She was just too tired, and declared that it was going to be an early night for both of them. Eight PM wasn't too early, and besides, she'd still get up before her regular five-thirty alarm.

The inflatable bed seemed to befuddle Al. Obviously, he'd never seen such a thing. The pump blew up the mattress quickly, and Sam knew that it was comfortable enough.

Well, maybe not for an elf used to a down-filled mattress and satin sheets, or whatever his kind generally slept in. Or maybe he spent his nights sleeping on woven branches in a tree.

This would just have to do for the evening.

Though Sam felt silly doing so, she still closed the door to her bedroom after saying goodnight. It wasn't as if she needed protection from Al. She justified shutting them, telling herself that he was the one who needed the privacy.

While it might actually have been she who needed some time alone with her thoughts.

She'd painted the bedroom walls a raspberry-sherbet color as a way of keeping the place dark. Blackout drapes made from deep green cloth covered the window. The bed was on one side of the long, skinny room, with the window at her feet and the closet at her head. It wasn't big enough for a queen-sized bed. She'd found a gorgeous bird's-eye maple twin bedframe that someone had committed the unforgivable sin of painting an ugly baby blue. Once she'd refinished it, it had served her well.

Sam had anticipated climbing into bed, under the hand-made quilt that Pedro's wife, Allysa had made, and dropping immediately off to sleep, as she normally did.

However, her life had just changed too much. Too many thoughts chased their way across her brain. Plus, it was far before her usual bedtime.

Why had Grandma Starling chosen her, and not Morgan? Had it been because of that machine he had?

He hadn't just picked it up. No, chances were, he'd had that machine for a while, and had used it before now.

Witches were the oath keepers, the portal keepers. While there wasn't a huge problem with monsters and the like creeping into the earthly plane, it was always a consideration.

Warlocks, on the other hand, were the oath breakers. They stole magic from witches and other places.

Had Morgan turned into a warlock? Most warlocks that Sam had heard about were the monsters on the netherplanes. While wasn't unheard of for a human witch to become a warlock, it was rare.

It was a serious enough accusation that Sam couldn't just fling it in his face. Had he turned away from being a witch and become a warlock instead? She didn't really know him that well. He was five years her senior, and they'd never shared schools or teachers, particularly not after Sam's disability had come to light.

He'd teased her as kids do, calling her an imbecile and making up stories about how she'd been dropped on her head as a baby. He'd never been there for her, never acted like a big brother to her. Tami's brother Phil had filled that role, being her protector a couple of times at school when she'd been bullied.

By the time she was twelve, Morgan had already left the house, going off to Harvard for business. He hadn't tortured her mercilessly as a kid. Honestly, he'd just mostly ignored her. She'd returned the favor, particularly as any time her parents had compared the two of them, she always ended up the worse of the two.

But she'd destroyed the machine he'd been using. Had that been the only way he'd be able to steal magic? Hopefully.

She'd have to keep an eye on him. But if he'd actually become a warlock, then it made more sense that the portal would choose her over him.

Why not any of the other cousins though? She could

understand why the portal hadn't wanted either Twee-dledumb or Tweedledumber. But her dad was also a witch, and had both a brother and a sister, who also had kids, all of whom had some level of magic.

No, there had to be something else at play, though she had no idea what it was.

And what about Al? She had to admit that the damned elf was growing on her. She'd be sad when he left, as he was sure to do once the council got around to appointing someone else.

Al had been on the human plane for quite some time, though. He was probably anxious to get back to his regular life. To being an important person again. He'd mentioned starting his campaign to become part of the council. Probably now that he'd done his duty here, he'd earned enough brownie points (elf points?) to have won his spot.

Then there was her job at the woodworking shop, which she loved. Was she going to have to leave that? Stick around the mansion the entire time? Grandma Starling had rarely left. All the family gatherings had gone to her instead.

Sam wasn't a homebody. She was going to get really resentful of her duty if she had to be. Especially that far from all the exciting things she could do downtown.

And what exactly had Grandma Starling done with her time? Sam knew she'd gardened. In addition to the roses, there was a pretty significant herb garden. However, Sam had a black thumb. Even plants that were supposed to be difficult to kill, like mint, died under her tender ministrations.

She knew that a lot of people depended on the portal for regular transportation between the planes. Having to meet and greet people constantly coming in and out of the portal was going to get really old, really fast.

What did Sam want to do for the rest of her life? Who did she want to be when she grew up?

She'd been fairly happy and content with herself and her situation.

Now what?

Still discontent, Sam finally felt herself slipping into sleep.

Unsurprisingly, a nightmare woke her.

She dreamed she was there, in her condo, in her bed, safe and warm.

A sound had disturbed her, though.

The sound of gnawing.

Damn it! The building had never had a problem with rats or mice. Insects, yes. Particularly when the old man who had lived above her had started going senile. He'd left food rotting on his kitchen counters. His condo had become infested with gnats who had then found their way to other dwellings.

But this noise—this was the sound of a rat, chewing wood.

In the dream, Sam got out of her bed and checked the closet. Instead of her clothes there was a large stack of wood planks. She had to go through each one, board by board, finding fecal evidence of rats or mice, and even a couple of pieces of wood infected with termites.

It was gross, exacting work, cleaning off each board, then stacking it to the side.

She felt herself growing more tense as the pile of wood in front of her diminished. She was going to have to face whatever was gnawing by the time she reached the bottom.

It was getting closer and closer. Maybe she'd missed something, and the rats had already escaped, and were now gnawing on her furniture?

Before Sam reached the bottom of the pile she woke herself up, out of the dream, sitting up in her bed.

The sound of gnawing still echoed in her ears.

What the hell?

She looked around, making herself look back at her closet. Though the doors were closed, she knew everything was fine there.

She could practically *feel* the gnawing, though.

Something was gnawing wood nearby.

Wait.

No.

Not here.

On the *mansion*.

It was 2:38 AM.

While a part of her wanted to climb back under the covers and deal with the issue in the morning, she knew she couldn't.

No, this was a threat she needed to face right now.

Particularly since that noise, though only in her head, was *so goddamned annoying*.

Sam slipped back on her jeans, though she put a warm gray hoodie on over that, with thick wool socks.

When she went out to the living room, Al was already awake and dressed. Sam didn't know if he'd ever gotten undressed or had just gone to sleep in his suit. Regardless, he still looked perfectly put together, like an overpaid lawyer who preyed on rich widows. Every hair on his head was already coiffed.

Al just looked at her when she stepped into the room, waiting for her to say something.

Was she in charge? Probably.

"There's something attacking the mansion," Sam told him, already cross with the world. "Rats, or something."

Al nodded thoughtfully. He hesitated, but Sam nodded at him.

She wasn't sure how this whole "portal keeper and protector" worked. But Al was probably used to her grandmother, who wouldn't have ever welcomed any advice.

"Is it inside the mansion? Or outside?" Al asked.

"Outside," Sam replied immediately. She didn't know how she knew, but she did.

After another pause, as Al looked at her expectantly, he finally said, "Then we shouldn't use your original portal, but a second one, that goes outside."

"Yeah, you're right," Sam said.

Al blinked, obviously surprised that she'd agreed so readily.

Again, the difference between her and her grandmother, who'd probably always insisted on being right, as well as the one to order everyone around and organize things.

"I'll make the second portal," Al said. He waved his

hand in the air, as if outlining a large oval with his palm, ending with a twisting flourish.

A new portal sprang up. It had less of a physical appearance than a metaphysical one. Sam could barely see it with her eyes, just a slight distortion of the background behind it. But she felt it, a sucking presence wavering in the middle of her living room.

Without saying anything more, Al walked through the portal.

Sam sighed and followed.

Going through an elven portal was different than a human one.

Any portal that Sam had ever traversed had been like taking a cool step through a doorway.

The elven one felt as though it lasted longer, like passing along a short hallway. Colors impinged on her sight, almost blinding her. The scent was like nothing she'd ever experienced before, like Chinese Five-Spice seasoning mingled with an exotic citrus.

She came out the other side shaking her head, trying to clear her vision and her senses.

They stood on the far side of the circular driveway in front of the mansion, just under the cover of the trees. Chances were, unless a creature had excellent night vision, it wouldn't see them there.

Sam had known that there would be rats attacking the mansion. She'd been imagining maybe a dozen or so.

The number appeared to be correct.

She'd gotten the scale all wrong, though.

These rats weren't really rats. They were monsters

from some netherworld, with just enough rat-shaped for her brain to associate them with rodents from the earthly plane. Even in the dark she could tell their mangy fur was gray. They had long snouts and massive teeth, scrawny, scaly legs ending in broken yellow claws, and a naked tail.

However, each was the size of a pony. Maybe four feet tall through the shoulders.

Shit.

How was she supposed to defend against them? She supposed that the house had natural defenses, ones she hadn't learned about.

Would it be easier for her to defend the house if they were inside of it? Or would the sound of the gnawing, which was setting her back up more and more, make her crazier if she was surrounded by it?

"What do we do?" Sam whispered to Al.

He grimaced and shook his head. "They're attacking the mansion," he said.

Duh. She could see that for herself.

When he didn't say anything more, Sam finally prompted him, "And?"

"They aren't attacking the portal," Al pointed out. "Legally, I can't do anything. And if I did, well, the council would be sure to find out."

"Once those creatures eat their way through the walls, they'll attack the portal," Sam said.

Al shook his head. "Unlikely. By the time they've made their way through the wood, they'll have eaten their fill, and will likely move on to someplace else."

Sam opened her mouth and shut it again. Damn it!

She'd never hear the end of it if the mansion fell down around the portal on her first night's watch.

Though she supposed that was probably the point. She had no proof that Morgan had been the one who'd called up these creatures, sent them to attack the mansion. However, she wouldn't be surprised at all if he had, as a matter of proving just how unfit she was as a guardian.

"There has to be something you can do," Sam said, cajoling. "Some way we can bend the rules. Right?"

Even in the dimness of the night, Sam could tell that Al was horrified by the idea.

"No, we do not *bend the rules*," he said. "I am here to protect the portal. Nothing else."

"Right. Not me, personally. Just what I represent," Sam said, bitterness dripping from her words.

"Exactly," Al said. He glanced at her. "Nothing personal."

"Of course not. Just business," Sam snapped.

There had to be a way to get those damned rats away from the house before they damaged the wood even more, before they gnawed their way through.

But how?

A crazy idea came to Sam, she who had little to no imagination.

"You protect the portal, right?" she said, clarifying.

"Correct," Al said.

"Gotcha," Sam said. And now that she was the guardian, he protected that power as well.

He would, in the end, protect her if those damned rats came after her.

Sam remembered the purple, spiky power she'd siphoned away from the portal, when Tweedledumb and Tweedledumber had her in their meaty paws. She held out her hand as she had then, thinking about the feeling of the power slapping against her palm, like icy rain.

There it was. Stinging harder this time, as though it were made from tiny bits of frozen hail.

Sam sucked in as much power as she could. Al merely watched her from the side. She couldn't tell if he was horrified or snickering at her.

Possibly a bit of both.

He had no idea what she could do when she got angry enough. To be honest, though, neither did she.

Instead of making the power rise back up and infuse her skin like a bug zapper, Sam stepped forward and pointed a finger at the first creature, imagining that golden lightning shooting out again, as it had the first time, killing Morgan's machine.

Nothing happened.

"What are you doing?" Al asked. He sounded exasperated.

"Stopping those monsters from attacking my home," Sam said. Though it wasn't her home, it still was in a way.

Besides, she *hated* rats, and how they gnawed at good wood, ruining it.

Sam marched forward across the yard. The creatures ignored her, focusing on their treat. Al stayed where he was. Coward. Shouldn't he at least be accompanying her, to make sure she was safe?

Or was he so certain that she'd fail?

Sam pushed away all thoughts of him, as well as the monsters on either side of the porch who gnawed on the corners, and focused on the mansion.

Could she electrify the walls? She knew how an electric fence worked. Could she put that same sort of wire running through the wood? Between the planks? Or else somehow infuse the boards?

Originally, she thought that the shape of the spell would be a long wire. That didn't do anything, though.

However, she'd used a wireman's wrench, specially designed for pulling wire through wood.

It looked kind of like tile snippers, with handles on one side and a flat end on the other that wire could be grasped with.

She imagined the shape of that tool in her head, filled it with magic and the cool smell of tin and aluminum, then *pulled*, first on one side of the porch, then the other.

A magical line formed, lighting up the base of the house, then along the uprights, outlining the foundation. Slowly, it started filling in the spaces in between.

Loud zaps filled the air as the power worked its way to the creatures who were breaking the line.

It was working! The sound of gnawing abruptly ceased.

Crap.

It was working. The monsters on either side of the porch now turned to her. She was probably glowing with magic still, particularly since she'd just been using it.

Sam backed away slowly, the monsters shuffling toward her.

"Do you need to wait until they actually attack me before you can start slaying them?" Sam asked as she got to the far side of the driveway.

Al obviously didn't put as much emotion into this sigh as he had been. She'd give him a low score for it.

"Oh, I could wait," he told her. "But since you obviously don't have a clue about what you're doing, I suppose I'll dive in now."

He had that glowing sword in his hands again. Damn, that thing was bright. Blindingly so.

Then the first creature attacked.

TEN

SAM HAD KNOWN that rats were gross.

Dead monster rats from one of the netherworlds?

Fucking impossibly gross.

Instead of blood, they'd been filled with a viscous, yellow fluid that stank worse than skunk cabbage and corpse flowers combined.

Every time Al had pierced one with his sword, the damned thing had exploded, showering them both with that awful goo.

At least she'd had the opportunity to see the elf disheveled, his perfect hair coated with slime, his suit stained beyond recognition.

However, she'd paid a high price for the privilege, as she was now coated with gunk as well.

The fight hadn't lasted too long. Al and his fancy sword had danced between the monsters, skewering them left and right. She'd managed to get in a few lightning strikes as well, though she'd had to get almost close enough to touch one before the magic would arc across from her outstretched hand to its mangy hide. Possibly they had some sort of resistance to magic. She'd have to remember to look it up in the bestiary sometime.

Now, Sam and Al sat on the front porch, looking out on the pile of horrible, dead bodies. Sam didn't want to move. The power she'd used had drained back into the house. She'd gladly let it go, willing it to infuse the mansion walls, granting them more protection.

Al sat beside her unmoving. Had he just made the fight look easy? Was he not moving because he was actually exhausted? Or was he so grossed out by the bodily fluids he was wearing that he didn't want to move?

"We should get cleaned up," Sam said.

Al nodded and waved his hand.

All the gore and nasty yellow fluid that coated them vanished. As did the bodies. He looked perfectly put together again, as always.

Sam blinked, surprised. "I'm not sure what you just did or where you sent those things, but thank you."

Al glanced at her and gave her a tight smile. "You're welcome," he said softly.

"What is it?" Sam asked.

"Those creatures cannot create a portal on their own. They're stupid. Something led them here. Directly to the mansion," he said.

"I know," Sam said. She sighed. "It was probably my brother." He was the best candidate in her book, in terms of wanting what she had.

Al shook his head. "No. They have a decidedly unearthly flavor to them. They wouldn't have listened to a human."

Sam shrugged. "So he got someone else to do his dirty work." Probably wasn't the first time and wouldn't be the last.

Al peered at her. "While I understand family rivalry, if it was indeed your brother, he should be dealt with."

"I can't prove it was him," Sam said. "But he's the one who really wanted the portal. He's the one who trained for it. Knows more about the damned thing than I do."

Al looked out into the night again. "If it was him, he'll attack you again," he warned.

Sam nodded. "And again, and again, until either I fall, or I can prove that he's the one behind the attacks."

"Then what?" Al asked. "There is no human equivalent of the high council."

"I...I don't know," Sam said. "The family would have to deal with him, I guess." Though what would that mean? Would they kill him? Would she have to kill him? That seemed like way too extreme of a solution. He was her *brother*. Couldn't he be redeemed?

"I cannot harm him," Al said. "For an elf to kill a human...it isn't allowed. And we *do* have a high council who would deal with me."

"Would they kill you?" Sam said, wanting to know the worst.

"Possibly," Al said. He shrugged. "Even if it was clearly a case of self-defense, they'd still think it was a fatal flaw in me, for not being able to defend myself from a lowly earth being."

"What if he's a warlock and has enhanced himself with power from other creatures?" Sam said.

"Even then," Al said. "They might banish me and forbid me from ever returning to the elven realms, if he proved himself to be that powerful."

"Would that be so bad?" Sam said.

"Imagine if someone took a torch to these woods," Al said softly. "Burned everything down, then salted the earth so nothing would grow back. How would you feel?"

"Gutted," Sam admitted. The trees—she had to admit they attracted her almost as much as the portal at this point.

"That wound would never heal," Al said. "That's how never going back to the elven world would be for me. A raw sore that would always bleed."

Sam heard the words unspoken: a wound that would possibly grow infected, and eventually would kill Al.

"Then we'll have to make sure that you don't end up having to deal with Morgan when it comes to it," she said.

Al just nodded thoughtfully and continued to stare out into the night.

It was not yet four AM. Sam was exhausted, but at the same time, she couldn't sleep. Something tickled at the back of her mind.

Sam stood, stretched, and went over to examine the damage the rats had done to the corner of the mansion.

They hadn't chewed their way through the outer

walls to the inner, though they'd been close. Hadn't bitten into any of the electrical wiring either.

She carefully brushed her fingers against the chewed off wood, avoiding giving herself a splinter, at least for now. The hole was obvious, maybe eighteen inches across, but only about six inches high. When her mother showed up, she was going to give Sam hell.

But not if Sam fixed it first.

Sam put her hands flat on the wood on either side of the hole. She could still feel the spiky purple magic flowing through the base of the house.

How could she fix this? What sort of magic could she use? Once daylight came, she could get wood to patch the hole. However, what could she do in the meanwhile?

Sam thought about the nature of the wood under her fingertips. It was old. Not just in the time that it had been attached to the mansion. The boards came from the Douglas firs found on the property. Not quite old-growth, but not young, either.

This wood had survived many storms even before being turned into lumber, as well as woodpeckers poking holes in it and the occasional rat gnawing at its roots. It had endured, and would endure for a long while. Not because that was the nature of this wood—Douglas fir was actually fairly soft. But because it still had youth singing in its veins, the magic keeping it young.

Sam removed her hands and thought about it for a few moments. She knew how trees grew. Had felt them before, particularly when she'd let the wood boards at the shop talk to her.

Layer upon layer, ring upon ring, the wood sprouted up.

She put her hands back on the wall, on either side of the hole. Trees never talked in words, but in songs. In her head, she started singing to the wood of the spring all around them, how strong the trees grew, how hardy and green the heart of the tree still was.

What little energy Sam had drained into the walls of the mansion. Sam sucked up power from beneath her feet, at the base of the house, and cycled it back through her hands.

Slowly, inch by inch, the wood began to grow, closing the hole in front of her.

This was magic of a different sort. It wasn't the same as the regular portal magic, or the spells that a witch normally formed. This was slow magic, earth magic. Sam wasn't really doing most of the work. Instead, she was just providing the power for the wood to heal itself, to grow back together, for the board's splintered ends to slowly intertwine and meld into a solid piece. The smell of the newly cut pine refreshed her. Her palms tingled with the magic flowing under them.

When the hole was finally closed, Sam felt the power in the mansion spike hard. That small hole had been draining a huge amount of magic away from the house and the portal inside.

The exterior walls created a type of circuit. Even a small hole disrupted that.

She stepped back and examined her work. She couldn't see in the dark, unlike said elf over there who appeared to be communing with the trees while seated on the porch, thinking deep elfy thoughts. Instead of using her eyes, she ran her fingers along the boards, sensing the join, smoothing it out and brushing away the splinters until the wood felt more whole.

Was the color the same? Probably not. However, Sam knew stain. She quickly formed the image of a paint brush in her head. The smell was easy to conjure as well, of hot concrete baking in the sunlight and the dark, chemical scent of the stain itself. She waved her hand over the naked wood, covering it.

Finally, that corner of the house was finished to her satisfaction.

When she turned around, she saw that Al, though still seated on the porch, was now watching her.

"What is it?" she said, walking toward him.

The elf nodded at her. "I should introduce you to Eloheme," he said.

"Who?" Sam asked. Sure, she was tired, but she didn't recognize the name.

"Friend of mine," Al said. Then he grimaced. "Acquaintance, at least. She's a wood elf."

"Really?" Sam said. She'd been of the impression that the high elves and the wood elves didn't really intermingle much.

"You'd probably get along," Al said. Then he turned his gaze back out across the driveway. "You going to finish the rest of the house now?"

Sam wanted to say no. She was so tired.

However, those holes in the mansion walls gnawed at her, just like the rats who had made them.

"Yeah," she said. At least the next one was likely to be easier. Closing the first one had changed the energy pattern of the mansion, brought it down a pitch because it wasn't dealing with that huge hole in the wall.

She trudged over to the next damaged piece of wood and began again.

The second hole did take less effort to fix, and the work got progressively easier as she went along.

Stepping back from the last hole, she nearly ran into Al. She'd been so focused on shoring up the walls of the mansion that she hadn't noticed him coming up from behind her.

"You need to sleep now," Al said firmly.

Sam was about to protest. She wasn't that tired. She'd stayed up all night before, albeit not recently.

She opened her mouth to say something when she swayed. It was as if someone had cut all the strings holding her up.

Crap. Instead of replying, she yawned so widely she thought her face would crack in two.

She hadn't been this tired while she'd been working. What was up with that?

"The house was supporting you while you did your work," Al said as he slipped an arm under her shoulder.

She was going to protest about him touching her without permission. However, she was also aware that she would have fallen over without the support.

He turned them around and started walking toward the front of the house.

"We're going back to your condo, where you will hopefully sleep in peace for a few hours," Al said. "Before we come back here."

Sam nodded, barely able to keep her eyes open.

The sky above the trees was definitely lighter. How long had she been working?

The trip through the elven portal wasn't as bad this time. Then again, she didn't traverse it alone, but with Al beside her. He walked her directly into her bedroom, letting her fall gracelessly onto her bed.

"I can take it from here," Sam assured him as she started to unlace her work boots.

"Are you certain?" Al asked.

"I don't need you to take my clothes off for me," Sam snapped. "I can do that myself."

"As you wish," Al said. His sly grin made her wonder as he backed out of the room and shut the door.

Sam managed to remove the hoodie and jeans she was wearing before she crawled under the covers and sank into a deep sleep filled with tense dreams that fled when she finally opened her eyes to her angrily ringing phone.

"What?" she said when she finally managed to snag it. It was her mother.

"Didn't you check your email?" her mother demanded.

"No," Sam said. "You know I only check it once a week or so."

"Well, we have an appointment at the lawyer's office in an hour. For the reading of the will," her mother told her. "You need to be there."

"Fine," Sam said. "We'll be there."

She hung up and shook her head. At least it was close to ten AM. She'd gotten maybe five hours of sleep.

It wasn't enough. Though nothing would ever be enough for her to go and face her family.

She'd rather go battle the damned rats again.

ELEVEN

SAM AND AL used the portal she'd created the night before to go out to the mansion, then Al generated a new one, from the mansion to the underground parking garage of the lawyer's building. Sam could only create a portal to a place she'd been before, and she'd never been to this lawyer's office.

Evidently, Al had gone with Grandma Starling once a year, so he knew the place well.

"Why did I never see you, or meet you, before now?" Sam asked as they stood in the elevator, going up to the eleventh floor.

"Your grandmother was set in her ways," Al said, as if that explained everything.

"So?"

"Her *human* ways," Al finally said as the door binged open.

Sam wasn't certain exactly what that meant. How badly had Grandma Starling treated Al? Just because he wasn't human didn't mean that he was stupid, or that she should be ashamed of him. Had he always been kept locked away in the portal room?

Sooner or later, she and Al were going to have a long chat about what he did and how he'd been treated.

The lawyer's office was a masterpiece dedicated to tasteful generic furnishings. Soothing, sage-green walls, beige carpet, brown upholstered chairs, and paintings of pink lady slippers seamlessly faded into the background, designed to be quickly forgotten.

Sam and Al were immediately shown to a conference room where the rest of the family had already gathered: Mom, Dad, Morgan, all her aunts and uncles, as well as many of the cousins. Most of them were dressed in somber clothes. Even Morgan had given up his usual collegiate blazer for a dark brown suit jacket, though instead of a shirt he'd stuck with the off-white turtleneck.

After enduring hugs from too many of her relatives, as well as nasty glares from Morgan, his wife Laureen, Tweedledumb, and Tweedledumber, Sam finally was able to escape when the lawyer came in. Everyone sat around the conference table that took up much of the middle of the room. The windows faced north, overlooking quite a few new construction sites.

To her surprise, the lawyer was female. She wore a maroon power suit with a man's shirt, white, open at the collar, no tie. She would have given Al a run for the money in terms of exquisitely styled hair, and her makeup was restrained and perfectly applied to her white skin. A set of pearl earrings completed the look with a matching pearl necklace. All in all, she exuded power, the kind that came with too much money and schooling.

It made sense. Since the lawyer was not a witch, she instead had oodles of the only other type of power that Sam's family would respect.

The lawyer introduced herself as Roberta Dion. After ensuring that everyone had everything they needed in terms of beverages, Roberta got down to business.

First, she checked everyone's ID herself, personally verifying that the only people in the room were on the list she carried in her papers. Even Al had a human-type ID. He'd also transformed himself using magic, so that he appeared human, disguising his ears and his eyes.

Then the lawyer pulled out the will. "As I'm certain many of you know, the will of Cecelia Starling is a bit unusual. No heir is listed by name. Instead, it states that the heir is to be determined by those family members who are present." Roberta glanced around the room, her eyes falling on Morgan.

Clearly, she also believed that Morgan would be declared the heir of the family.

However, everyone else was looking at Sam, until she finally spoke up.

"I am the heir," Sam said into the silence.

Roberta blinked, obviously surprised, but recovering quickly. "You are Samantha Dunham, correct?"

"I am," Sam said.

"Do the rest of you attest that Samantha Dunham is the heir to the estate of Cecelia Starling?" Roberta asked.

She went around the room, and one by one, every member of the family conceded that yes, Sam was the heir.

Even Morgan, though Sam could tell that the words stuck like dry sawdust in his throat.

Roberta asked to see Sam's ID again, copying off her information. "In addition to the estate, you are now the executor of the Starling Trust, which shall be renamed the Dunham Trust, as per Cecelia's instructions."

Sam nodded. She'd been expecting that.

"There are several conditions involved with being the executor," Roberta continued. "You must immediately sign and fill out your own will. For now, it will be identical to Cecelia Starling's original will, with details changed only after a year's time. Next, you will agree to meet with either me or my designated inheritor once a year to verify all instructions, the family members to meet upon your death and choose a new heir, as well as review the accounts."

She had Sam sign paperwork agreeing to those conditions.

The lawyer went on, talking about how much money Sam would have each month as her allowance, paid for by the trust.

Sam blanched. Damn. She really was rich now.

"There are also ways you can draw against the fund for specific expenses, such as mansion maintenance, taxes, and so on," Roberta said. She gave Sam a tight smile. "I know it's a lot to absorb right away. I will give you my personal number. Don't hesitate to call if you have any questions. I'm on retainer for your family. Feel free to use my time."

Sam nodded. It really was a lot. Was she going to have to read all these contracts? Go over the terms of the will? Her head hurt just thinking about it.

Fortunately, she was better with numbers than she was with letters. Normally, that wasn't the case when someone had dyslexia. However, Sam had to do fractions in her head all the damned time as part of her job, so she'd gotten much better with them.

"The rest of you may go at this point," Roberta said to the family. "Samantha and I have paperwork to fill out."

"We'll see you back at the mansion," Mom said imperiously.

Sam checked her watch. It was only ten thirty.

"I'll meet you all there this afternoon, at two PM," Sam said. She needed time to make sure that the repair work was all in place, that nothing looked odd about the house.

Mom looked startled that Sam had said anything at all. She opened her mouth to disagree, but surprisingly, Dad gave her a hard elbow to her side.

It wasn't good that her dad had never said anything before now. Still, Sam was happy that he was finally on her side. At least a little bit.

"Fine," Mom said. "We'll see you then."

With that, she swept out of the room, the rest of the relatives following in her wake.

Sam took a deep breath when they'd finally left, feeling as though the air had returned to the room.

"I need to print out a new copy of the will, with your name listed on the final page," Roberta said. "As well as bring in the notary to witness your signature." She left.

Al remained behind. Roberta didn't seem to think anything of it. Then again, she'd met Al before, he'd been there frequently with Grandma Starling.

Sam glanced back at Al.

He nodded, giving her a small smile. "You're doing fine," he assured her.

Sam shook her head. "It's still a lot to take in, you know?"

"Yes, it is," he said. "And we still need to talk about your duties as the gate guardian."

Sam grimaced. "I expected that. At least I told the family to not bother me until this afternoon. Want to make sure the house repairs are in order."

"Don't they feel right to you?" Al asked, sounding a bit alarmed.

"Yeah, well, I still want to see it," Sam said.

Al nodded but he looked puzzled.

Sam had never been able to do much magic. She'd certainly never learned to trust it. She felt much more comfortable doing things with her own hands.

Though, once she got the hang of it, she might be able to re-stain the entire mansion in an afternoon, using magic. Lighten up the wood.

And what could she do to the rest of the place?

The lawyer and the notary came back in the room before Sam got much of a start on reimagining the dark, stuffy rooms. She signed a bunch of paperwork, including signature cards so Sam could withdraw money from the accounts. The new bank card would be special delivered to the house the next morning.

There was *so much money.*

However, Roberta had instructed Sam that most of the money would stay in the account, set aside for future generations.

That was good, actually. Because otherwise, Sam might be tempted to immediately start a major renovation of the house.

Might do that anyway, just based on her own, personal income.

It turned out that the trust paid for her parents already, a separate account that she didn't control. So she couldn't yank at their purse strings.

Too bad.

"Does my brother, Morgan, also get money?" Sam had to ask. He made enough on his own with his investment firm. But he loved money more than just about anything.

Roberta shook her head. "No. Just the direct descendants of Cecelia Starling. Her daughters."

That meant Mom and Aunt Karen. Not her dad, or his siblings. And none of the cousins.

"Though the will doesn't stipulate that you must produce heirs, more money would be allocated to you if you do," Roberta said.

Sam nodded. She'd never thought about having a baby, not really. She didn't actually like kids. And while she might have, possibly, *occasionally*, entertained the idea over the last year or so while she'd been with her ex, before things got bad, she didn't have anyone in her life now.

They finished the paperwork finally, both standing up at the same time. Roberta stuck out her hand. "I'm serious about being able to call me at any time," the lawyer said firmly. "Whenever you feel out of your depths about the money. Or taxes. Or the inheritance." She gave a sharp smile. "Or if anyone in your family feels the need to badger you about money. Just send them my way."

"Thank you," Sam said. She was tempted to ask Roberta if she wanted to catch an early lunch together, but she really did need to get back to the mansion. It was drawing close to noon and she needed to check on everything, as well as eat, before the family descended on her.

Roberta paused, then said, "I will have my secretary call you in the next few days to set up our next appointment."

"Good," Sam said. "Let's meet in a couple of weeks." She had copies of the will to read at home, and now that she had a spell to actually *help* her read, she planned on going through the whole damned thing.

Along with the books that Al had picked out for her. And whatever else she needed to do.

Sam and Al left the office and rode the elevator silently back to the parking garage. Sam would bet that part of the reason why her grandmother had chosen this law firm was because of the underground parking lot. It had a lot of dark corners where one could easily blip in and out with no one noticing.

Sam immediately felt better as soon as they arrived on the estate. She was able to check her work, walking around the outside of the mansion, verifying that the color did match perfectly. She ran her fingers across the wood, noting how perfectly sealed the joins were. She could barely find them anymore. The wood not only had healed, it continued to heal. In another day, no one would find them.

She gave a huge sigh of relief at that.

One less thing to have to fight the family over.

Because she had a feeling that their next visit was sure to be another goddamned battle.

TWELVE

SAM HAD a similar salad to Al's, though hers had bacon and turkey on it while his did not. Otherwise, they were the same, with tasty butter lettuce, strawberries, orange slices, pecan pieces, and a sweet vinaigrette.

The restaurants out in Ravenswood had improved over the last few years. Gentrification was hitting the area hard. And while she hated seeing some of the farms and fields get turned into McMansions, it might not be the worst thing.

They'd gotten the food to go, and so sat in the kitchen again, though this time Sam was facing the rest of the house and Al was looking out the back windows.

Al obviously wasn't used to eating with someone, and had been a bit awkward when Sam had told him to sit down and join her. Had Grandma Starling insisted on her meals alone? Or that he serve her or some such nonsense?

"So, how does this whole portal guardian thing

work?" Sam asked as they finished up. Al had requested that they eat before they talk.

"On Mondays, Wednesdays, and Fridays, there are regular hours for the portal, when people can come through as they need to," Al said. "You will be expected to be in the portal room during those hours, generally from one PM to five PM. I will be on the elven side of the portal at that time."

"All right," Sam said. Didn't sound too bad. Not too many hours. But it did sound as though she was going to have to quit her real job. She wasn't looking forward to telling Juan or talking with her shop steward.

She'd just have to make a point of visiting them. Or perhaps inviting them out to the mansion…

"There are other times when people will need to access the portal," Al continued. "Mostly that's done by arrangement, but occasionally something will come up. You'll feel the portal when someone requests to come through."

"Can they just pass through the portal? Without asking permission first?" Sam asked.

"It's possible, yes," Al said. "You can instruct the portal to allow anyone to pass through. However, I would advise against it. You don't want people just arriving here without forewarning."

Sam nodded. That made sense. One additional precaution, even though there were guards on the elven side. As part of what little magical training she'd received, she had been taught about the portals, and the dangers of having an unguarded one. There were too many beasts and monsters in the netherworlds who considered humans a tasty treat.

"All traffic through the portal has been halted for a week while we dealt with the death of your grandmother," Al said. "My hope is that you and I can train for the rest of this week, and you can get familiar with the portal and how it works, so that we can open it again next week."

Sam nodded. It was already Wednesday, though it felt as though as week had passed since Grandma Starling had died. When were they going to hold the memorial service? She supposed that was part of why her mother wanted to call the family together. Was there some other ritual that happened when a witch died? She didn't recall anything like that when Grandpa Starling had died. Then again, he hadn't been a witch.

"How much traffic goes through the portal?" Sam asked, curious.

"Well, some people live in the elven realms, but do much business here. A lot of wood elves," Al said. "Mondays and Fridays are the busiest times."

"So, they come here, then create their own portal off the property?" Sam said, still trying to get a feeling for how this all worked. She couldn't imagine that anyone arriving here would then call for an Uber or something. That would be noticed by humans and remarked on. Whereas witches needed to operate under the radar at all times, at all costs. That had been drilled into Sam early.

"Yes. Though they can't set one up in the portal room," Al said. "No one can create a portal in the portal room, a second portal, that is."

"That's why there's a mudroom directly opposite the portal door!" Sam said, the mystery figured out. "The family never uses it."

Al peered at her. "You didn't know that was the second portal room?" he asked, confused.

Sam shrugged. "Why should I? No one told me much about magic at all, or what my family did."

"As you surmised, the mudroom, as you call it, is the second portal room, where visitors come and go from the property," Al said. "There are spells that you'll have to renew, protecting that space as well."

"Okay, so I take care of the portal, greet visitors, escort them on and off the property. Renew the spells as necessary. What the hell else am I supposed to do? What did Grandma Starling do with her time?" Sam asked.

"Your grandmother spent a lot of time researching spells," Al said in the driest tone that Sam had ever heard. "Coming up with new systems of categorization. You'll find a lot of her journals in the portal room."

Sounded like a lot of busy work. And Sam would bet that Al hadn't approved of any of it.

"Probably not going to be my forte," Sam said. Spending all her time reading and writing sounded like sheer hell to her.

"You might be able to create a spell that would write out the words for you," Al pointed out.

Still sounded like hell.

"What else did Grandma Starling do?" Sam asked.

"She spent time in her garden," Al said.

"I've never had any luck growing things," Sam admitted.

"Really?" Al said, surprised. "I would have thought that was something you'd excel at. Strange."

Sam fidgeted under his close scrutiny. She'd always killed houseplants.

Then again, a scrawny mint plant wasn't a tree.

"I'll figure it out," Sam promised him. "And I'll study hard," she added. She didn't want to make her family proud. Those assholes could all drop off the face of earth and she probably wouldn't miss them much.

However, she'd always taken pride in her work. Just because the nature of her job had changed dramatically didn't mean that she still couldn't do her best at it.

And who knew? Maybe being a portal guardian would bring her joy someday.

Maybe even as much joy as properly fitting dove-tailed corners.

CHAPTER

THIRTEEN

OF COURSE, Mom was the first to arrive.

Luckily, Sam was expecting it. She had opened the door to the mudroom so it would be easy for people to come into the house. She'd also bought refreshments for people to eat. She remembered that Grandma Starling had done a lot of her own cooking. For this afternoon, Sam had bought what her ex had always called "deconstructed salad"—also known as a veggie tray. She'd also gotten a cheese and meat tray, some sourdough bread that had smelled heavenly, and whipped up a batch of garlic butter that even Al had deigned to declare was passable.

"I'm in the kitchen!" she called out when she *felt* her mom arrive.

It was strange how her senses had expanded. She knew which room Al was in (currently on the front porch doing that communing with the trees thing) and she could always feel the portal.

According to Al, her senses needed to be further

tuned, but that was a task for the following weeks. He thought it would take a full year for her to be trained, not just attuned to the property but to discover how she would work with the portal.

The bright May sunshine had remained, and Sam had opened up the windows over the sink just to smell the fresh air. The weather was unpredictable, though, so it wouldn't surprise her if there were showers before the end of the day.

Sam had set all the food out on the large cooking island in the middle of the kitchen, with various bottles of water, soda, wine and beer on the breakfast bar.

Mom glanced around the kitchen, obviously surprised. "You didn't have to go to all this trouble," she said as she came over to face Sam.

Sam shrugged. "Figured any sort of family gathering would go more smoothly with food."

Mom gave Sam a cool appraising look. "I happen to agree with you," she said. "I'm just surprised that you thought of it."

"So what do you want, Mom?" Sam said, rather than reply to the implication that she was stupid in all ways.

"I take it you've already started your training with the portal," Mom said as she walked over and poured herself a glass of merlot.

"Yes," Sam said. She wasn't about to go into the details or to admit that she'd barely done anything since the rat attack.

"How?" Mom asked, turning back to Sam and nailing her point blank. "How are you able to do any training? You can't read."

Sam gave her mother a brittle smile. "Of course I can read, though no thanks to you. You've heard of audiobooks, right?"

"The tomes you need to study don't have an audio version," her mother said dismissively.

"They do if you apply the right magic to them," Sam said. "Luckily, I'd discovered that spell a few years ago."

Al had said that she could never admit that he'd taught her the spell.

"I beg your pardon?" Mom said, her eyes growing wide. "What spell?"

"Books want to be read, you know," Sam said. "All you have to do is nudge them the right way, and they'll read themselves to you."

Mom's eyes narrowed at her. "That's not possible."

"I assure you, it is," Sam said.

Mom shook her head. "Oh, I know the spell. You couldn't have just picked that up on your own, though. Someone must have taught you."

Al unfortunately came into the kitchen at that moment.

"You!" Mom said, rounding on the elf. "You've been interfering again, haven't you? Grandma always said you were a busybody."

"I have no idea what you're speaking of," Al said at his haughtiest.

"You taught her how to use a reading spell, so she could get through her training," Mom accused Al.

"I already told you, he didn't," Sam interjected before Al could say anything. "I learned that spell myself. Years ago. Don't you remember me lamenting that I couldn't find audiobooks for some older books? That I was going to have to create them myself?"

Her mother pulled herself up stiffly before turning to face Sam. Her face was completely void of expression. "I do remember that. And that you were experimenting with some program but you couldn't get it to work right. The voice sounded unnatural."

"Exactly," Sam said. "So I tried figuring out if I could do it myself."

Mom peered at her. "I think you're lying to me. I think *he* taught you. But I'm not going to argue about it. Not now."

Sam nodded. She hadn't won this round. The topic had just been shelved until a later date, when her mother was certain to accuse her of lying again.

"What kind of memorial service should we organize?" Sam said, changing the subject.

"Though your grandmother was raised in a church, she wasn't a regular church goer," Mom said. "She didn't have many beliefs, and she certainly didn't believe in the Goddess."

Sam pressed her lips together in an effort to not roll her eyes at her mother and her beliefs. Sam had speculated more than once that because her mother had a deity in her life, it had probably softened her outlook some, and that she'd be completely amoral without those guiding principles.

They started talking details—having a gathering out there on the property in the backyard sometime the following week. Sam would have to rent pavilions and a catering service. Luckily, her mother had the details of the company that Grandma Starling had used every time the family had gathered.

That extra money was going to come in handy if Sam was now required to host all the family gatherings.

She'd be certain to invite Roberta. Though the lawyer probably hadn't been that friendly with her grandmother, Sam knew she'd still want to come and pay her respects. As well as to talk more with Sam about things.

Plus, it would probably put her mother's back up some. Not that Sam was constantly looking for things to do that would upset her family...

The rest of the family arrived shortly afterward. No one bothered driving. They all came via portal.

It probably was just coincidence that Morgan arrived directly after Aunt Karen, Tweedledumb, and Tweedledumber. They hadn't all been meeting together.

Right?

There ended up being sixteen people total, between the aunts, uncles, and cousins. None of the grand-nephews or nieces had come along, or there would have been nearly thirty people at the gathering. Sam was particularly happy that Morgan's insipid wife and three hellions weren't there. While his wife Laureen would have tried to smother her (again) in fake sympathy, the kids would have attempted to burn the house down, given half a chance.

After everyone grabbed a plate of food, Mom ushered them into the stiff living room. Tall windows at the front overlooked the driveway. Another fireplace graced this space, on the side wall between the windows there. It was one of the few working fireplaces in the house, as most of them had been replaced with gas. Gray and reddish-brown tile made up the mantle, probably original to the house, but still ugly and dark. An awkward painting of Grandma Starling's parents took up the space above the mantle.

White-painted bead-wood wainscoting covered the lower portion of the walls. A dark green wallpaper with a tiny pattern of lighter green leaves took up the top portion, all the way to the high ceilings. Though it was old fashioned, Sam wouldn't replace it immediately.

Probably.

Despite the tall windows, the space seemed dark and dim. The sofa and chairs all matched each other, with carved rosewood arms and legs and red and brown upholstery. The rugs were all red and brown as well, hiding the nice wooden floors.

Sam was going to have to revamp the entire space if she was ever going to feel comfortable in here.

Morgan sat on the couch closest to the fireplace beside Aunt Karen. Tweedledumb and Tweedledumber sat opposite them. The rest of the family had pulled in chairs from either the kitchen or one of the studies, and they all sat in a rough circle, with Sam and her mom sitting together opposite the fireplace. Al stood behind her, somewhere to her left.

At first, Mom and Sam talked about the memorial service they'd started planning for the following Thursday. Aunt Karen volunteered to contact some of Grandma Starling's other friends to inform them about the death as well as the service. Seemed her grandmother had been the head of a gardening club out here.

As soon as that topic wound its way down, the energy in the room shifted abruptly. Sam would swear that the temperature had just dropped five degrees.

"As we all know, Sam is now the heir to the Starling portal," Mom started off with.

Sam blinked, surprised. She'd never heard it called that. Al had always referred to it as the Choowe portal. Was that the elvish name for it?

Morgan piped up. "We should rename it to the Dunham portal."

"I'd heard it was called the Choowe portal," Sam said. She knew that she might be sticking her foot in it, but she was supposed to be learning everything, right? And the best way to learn was to make mistakes. She'd figured that out early on, particularly after she'd started trying new types of art.

You couldn't expect to make a perfect pot the first time you sat down at a wheel.

"That is not appropriate," her mother said, throwing a glare at Al for good measure.

His still standing position allowed him to naturally look down his nose at everyone.

"Why not?" Sam asked, aiming for innocence though she probably missed the mark, given how her mother transferred her glare to her.

"That is the local name for the portal," her mother said dismissively.

"What do you mean, local?" Sam asked, honestly confused now.

"This was always a place of power," Morgan said, using a lecturing tone. "Before the portal was consecrated and dedicated to our use."

"So you're saying that it's the local tribe's name for this place?" Sam said. "Before us white people took it over?"

At least her mother had the ability to look a little uncomfortable at that. "Honestly, Sam, it doesn't matter."

"If it doesn't matter, then we should use the local name for it," Sam said brightly. "I propose we rename the portal the Choowe portal, and that name should be constant. Not changing with every portal keeper."

"No one outside of the family will use that term," Mom warned.

Sam shrugged. "As you said, it doesn't matter. So let's just name it appropriately, once and for all. Shall we?"

Mom narrowed her eyes at Sam. "Very well. Since you're determined to have your way in matters that you do not even begin to comprehend. We shall now call it the Choowe portal."

"Great!" Sam said. She stood up. "Since we've taken care of all the business now, shall we get on with the rest of the socializing?"

"That isn't all the business we needed to discuss," her mother said primly. "There's still the matter of your training."

"I thought Al was going to handle that," Sam said. At their blank looks, she added, "You know. Alanthin

Himladhon. The elf." She waved a hand in his direction. "Along with all the books I'll have to read."

"Alanthin isn't an appropriate teacher," Mom said.

"So are *you* going to come and teach me now?" Sam said. She couldn't help the bitter tone that crept into her voice.

Her mother, the one who'd declared that teaching Sam anything was a waste of time?

"No. I propose that Morgan be your teacher," Mom said.

Aunt Karen spoke up. "I agree. Morgan was supposed to be the heir of the Dunham portal." She held her chin up, looking mulishly stubborn. "He's the one with most of the knowledge of its workings."

"Plus, there are the dignitaries. People you've never met. Who Morgan already knows and has relationships with," Mom said.

Sam sank back down into her chair. She knew it was a bad idea to allow Morgan to get any closer.

However, if he was here, working with her, would he stop attacking the mansion?

"I'm certain that Alanthin can introduce me to everyone I need to know," Sam said.

"He'll only know of some of the alliances," Aunt Karen said. "He won't understand the significance of their relationships. Their *human* allies."

Sam threw a questioning glance back at Al. She was pretty certain that he'd know, or at least be aware of, the network of dealings between all the important personages.

Al gave her a cool look, as if to indicate that such dealings were far beneath him.

They might have been. Then again, perhaps Grandma Starling had kept Al at arm's length, away from any of the human arrangements.

"In addition, Morgan has the best working knowledge of the portal," Mom said. "While you may have some innate abilities, you're in far above your head."

"You don't think I can figure it out?" Sam asked frostily.

"No, I don't," her mother said frankly. She stared hard at Sam. "I'm afraid that you're going to blunder and fail. Not at first. But you're going to go in too deep. You always did, as a girl. The portal will call to you, and you'll enter, never planning on exiting or returning. You're already having problems ignoring the portal. You're constantly looking over your shoulder at it."

Sam shook her head, startled. Sure, the portal impinged on her attention. But that was always going to be the case. She'd get used to it. Right?

"This was why we wanted you to share that power," Morgan said, sounding reasonable for once and not like a snotty professor. "So that you'd have a chance against the pull of the portal."

Sam threw another look at Al, but he didn't even meet her eyes, instead, staring off into the distance, removing himself from the conversation.

"Would you have given up the power, once you had it?" Sam demanded, turning on Morgan.

"Of course he would have," Aunt Karen chided. "How could you accuse him of being a warlock?"

Sam opened her mouth, then shut it again. "Wasn't it a little convenient that he had that device, all ready and working, wouldn't you say?" she asked.

No one answered.

"We can't force his help on you," Mom said quietly beside her. "It would certainly go a long way to easing our worries if you'd accept it, though. Taking guidance from your family, for once, rather than striking off on your own foolish quest. Or listening to someone who isn't even human."

Sam rolled her eyes at that, though she did hear the truth behind her mother's words. While Al wasn't human, he certainly had the portal's best interests at heart. Didn't he?

However, he'd also made it clear to her that he was here to protect the human side of the *portal*. The power she represented. Not her, personally.

"What can you teach me about the portal that I can't figure out myself, or learn from books?" Sam asked Morgan directly.

Morgan sat for a moment. Sam gave him the benefit of the doubt that he was considering his answer, and not just pausing for dramatic effect.

"The Dunham portal does not exist in a vacuum," Morgan said.

Sam nearly rolled her eyes at that. Of course it wasn't singular. It was a *portal*. That meant it was connected to someplace else.

"Though its primary end is located in the elven plane, it passes through portal *space*, where all the other worlds are located. You know those golden lights that flicker on and off in the depths of the portal?" Morgan said, staring at Sam for confirmation that she'd actually seen them.

"The ones that look like fireflies. Yes," Sam said, nodding.

"Those are actually from the world Narderholt," Morgan continued. "Which means that it's currently the closest of the other worlds to this one, at least in portal space. They've only been seen in the Dunham portal for a few years. Eventually, they'll be replaced with something else, when Narderholt floats away and another world draws closer."

Sam considered. That probably wasn't something that would be in any of the books that she was reading, as they were all ancient.

"As part of your duties, you need to note the closest worlds to ours, when they arrive and depart," Morgan said.

"Is there a pattern to the shifting worlds? Some sort of orbit?" Sam asked.

Morgan looked frustrated. "Not that I've been able to figure out. That was one of the projects I wanted to continue working on, though. I've met with a few of the other working portal keepers, comparing notes. I think that if we could get all that data and maybe put it into a computer, we could determine the orbits of the other worlds, as well as our own."

"Huh," Sam said. She didn't know if that would actually be useful or not. She threw a glance at Al, but his expression basically said that he was above such trivia.

"All right," Sam said slowly. "I will allow you to help train me in the use of the Choowe portal."

Morgan gave her a triumphant smile. Aunt Karen looked smugly pleased as well.

"However," Sam said as she stood. "You will remember that this is *my* property. *My* house. *My* portal."

It didn't take much effort to reach out to the walls of the mansion. She *knew* them, knew the structure of the wood, how the planks lay, the strength of the studs. Knew where the nails were still square, where the plaster and lathe lay thick and heavy.

Underneath all that, buried deep into the foundation, Sam found that bright wire of power that she'd pulled through the walls earlier.

It wasn't some magic trick. She knew how an electric fence worked. She just upped the voltage, until the walls of the stuffy living room crackled with bright purple power. Slivers of lightning danced around the white window frames. Even the empty fireplace filled with magical flames.

It was like sitting inside a giant bug zapper.

Everyone looked startled at her display of power. Including Morgan.

Good.

Sam dropped the magic quickly, letting it sink back down into the foundation. She knew that her power was fairly limited, at least at this point. She'd been up half the night, then dealing with her family for much of the day. She was already exhausted, and it wouldn't take much before she was falling over again.

"Are we clear?" Sam asked in the nervous silence that followed.

"We are," her mother said primly from beside her. "And we're all suitably impressed with that little light show as well."

Sam turned to glare at her mother, who returned the look.

"It's obvious that I was mistaken, and that you do have some innate magical abilities," Mom said grudgingly.

She didn't sound sorry about her early judgments, though.

"It still remains to be seen, though, if that power of yours can be transferred to the delicate job of running the Dun—Choowe portal."

Sam wanted to ask her mom how much she wanted her daughter to fail. It wasn't the time or place.

For now, Sam had made her choice. Set her boundaries. And heaven help anyone who got in her way.

CHAPTER

FOURTEEN

AFTER THE FAMILY FINALLY LEFT, Sam had to search for a while before she found Al. Though he was still on the property, he was no longer in the mansion, but outside, all the way across the backyard, just under the first line of trees. The sky had turned darker and the air had a distinct chill to it now, as Sam had expected. It wasn't raining yet, but it would be soon.

Sam walked up to the elf cautiously. He stood with his hands behind his back, staring out among the trees, doing that communing thing again.

What did he see when he stared so hard? Was he seeing anything at all? Or was his vision taken up with memories? Other worlds, other places?

Al glanced over at Sam as she came to stand beside him, but he didn't say anything, looking back at the trees.

Salal bushes crowded around the base of each trunk, white flowers hanging down like tiny bells under the thick, broad leaves. Blackberry bramble took up the space just beyond. Several baby pine trees struggled to find space and light to grow. The air smelled of mulch and the coming rain.

It was darker standing here than she'd expected. Just that little bit of shade blocked the light.

Or these woods were particularly dim. There was always that as well. She'd never felt welcomed by these trees.

Taking over the portal hadn't changed that feeling.

"They're all gone," Sam told Al. Perhaps unnecessarily, though he had disappeared right after the family meeting in the living room.

Al nodded.

"So what's next?" Sam asked.

Al shrugged. "It's your house. Your portal. You tell me."

The tone wasn't even that snooty. He sounded more resigned than anything else.

Back to dealing with the emo teenager again.

Sam contained her sigh.

"What's that all about?" she asked.

"You don't need me. You have a teacher, now," Al pointed out.

Sam rolled her eyes. "Yes, one I don't trust."

"Then why did you accept his help?" Al said, finally turning to look at her.

"Haven't you ever heard, 'keep your friends close, but your enemies closer'?"

"That's a stupid saying," Al replied.

"But Morgan will know some things about the portal that you don't think are important," Sam said.

"Like plotting the courses of the pocket worlds?" Al sneered. "That's as useful as categorizing spells."

"Why is that?" she asked instead of pointing out that it might be useful for her to learn spells if they were organized in a fashion that made sense to her.

"The elves have been tracking the other nether-worlds for millennia," Al said. "The movement is random. No computer is going to find otherwise."

"But it will give Morgan something useless to do. Keep him out of our hair if he's chasing straws that way," Sam pointed out.

Al shook his head. "No, he's going to want *you* to chase straw that way. Loose bits of fluff that won't actually help you. He's going to waste your time."

"Good thing I strictly limited the number of hours that he'll be tolerated here on the estate," Sam said.

Al glanced over at her. "I wish you hadn't done it, though."

"I know," Sam said. "In a perfect world, I wouldn't have had to. But accepting his help also meant getting my family off my back, at least for a little while."

"You aren't close to your family," Al said. "Why bother to please them?"

"Because they *are* my family," Sam said. "While sure, I have a family of choice, the people I work with, my friends, they don't know anything about the magic. My bio-family are the only ones who do. I need to keep them around while I learn more."

Al gave a sigh that would score pretty low on the emo scale. He sounded more tired than anything else.

"I still think it's a mistake to grant your brother access to the estate at all," he said.

"We'll burn that bridge when we get to it," Sam promised. "Now, I'm going to spend a little time in the portal room, with the portal, then do a quick once-over of the entire mansion before I leave for the day."

"What?" Al snapped. "Why would you leave for the day? Why aren't you spending the night here? Remember what happened last night?"

"I know," Sam said. Her own sigh probably would have done any thirteen-year-old girl proud. "I just don't feel comfortable moving in here yet."

"And when will you feel comfortable?" Al asked archly.

"Mom and Aunt Karen are coming by tomorrow morning to help clean out some of Grandma Starling's things," Sam said. "Though I officially inherited everything, I know there's some of Grandma's jewelry that her daughters would like to have."

Al merely raised one cool eyebrow at that.

"So after we clean out some of Grandma Starling's belongings, then I can start bringing my things here," Sam continued. "I need to make space before I move in. Make some changes. Liven up the rooms. Maybe change out the windows."

Al's expression was a masterpiece of blank emotionless stillness.

Surely he knew that she could do the work herself, right? Or was that what he was afraid to comment on?

"Come on. Let's get back in the house before the rain starts," she said.

Al still hesitated. "Are you certain you want me to come with you?"

"Yes," Sam said immediately. "Look, I know, my mother doesn't trust you. The rest of the family looks down on you because you're not human. And I'm aware that you aren't here to personally protect *me*, but the power I represent." She paused, then went on. "But I trust you more than I trust my whole damn family, combined."

Al gave her a brittle smile. "Low bar," he commented.

Sam shrugged. "It's the best I can do for now."

And it was. She'd only known Al for a day now.

She was not looking forward to when he'd be leaving her, alone against everyone she knew.

FIFTEEN

Sam didn't want to say that she was obsessed with the portal.

No, really. She could walk away at any time.

However, it *did* constantly draw her attention. Since her mother had pointed it out, Sam realized that yes, indeed, she was always glancing over her shoulder, looking toward the room the portal was contained in.

It was a nervous tic she was going to have to break.

"All new portal keepers feel this way, right?" Sam asked as she led Al toward the portal room, her heart beating faster, her mood suddenly lifting.

It was as if she was going to meet a new lover, that tinge of excitement that flushed through her blood, made her stomach wobble.

"I've only ever met your grandmother, when she was a new keeper," Al said. "*She* certainly never acted like a giddy schoolgirl, whether she was around the portal or not."

Sam threw a glare at him but it bounced off, as usual.

Then, she was stepping through the plain door, into the portal room, and everything else fell away.

The portal didn't hum audibly to her. She felt the sound, deep in her bones, like the reverberations of a train passing by many miles away. The smell of homey soup and fresh bread came to her again, comforting scents that made her breathe more deeply, calming her racing heart.

It looked the same as it had the other day, with the four pillars surrounding a dark black mist. Small golden lights flashed at her—supposedly from the Narderholt world. Al had told her more about it, how there weren't any intelligent creatures there, and no sunlight either. Instead, it had a tremendous insect life, and all of it used bioluminescence as a way of finding one another.

Where were the purple lights from? Or were those always present? She would bet the latter, as they seemed to be part of the portal itself. They zinged merrily across the darkness, small jolts of joy.

Al didn't stand beside her, but went back to examine the bookshelves. Even though he could see in the dark, Sam still raised the lights up. She didn't even have to go back to the door this time to do it, but could just point her finger toward the space and flick the switch.

Sam braced herself, anticipating that the wood would grab at her, then reached out to touch one of the front pillars, the fluted pair that looked like they'd been made from golden burly-oak.

She couldn't feel the soul of the wood.

All she felt was the hard, smooth surface, which tingled with magic slightly under her fingertips.

The difference was underneath that. Most wood talked to Sam. Even wood that had been aged, like the boards of the house.

This wood didn't even whisper. Its voice had long since vanished.

It wasn't that the wood was dead. Even though it had been cut centuries (millennia?) ago, this column still lived and breathed.

But just barely.

Sam withdrew her hand, puzzled. She'd expected a much bigger response. She'd prepared herself to be drawn in, the wood longing to sing to her of its life.

This wood didn't, though.

"Al?" Sam asked as she stepped back.

"Hmm?"

"What can you tell me about these pillars? In particular, the wood they were made from?"

Al gave her a quick smile. It was almost friendly.

Then he fell into haughty lecture mode.

"These pillars came from trees of the Doladgathor," Al said. "There are none left of its kind. They grew together in a single valley, north of the High King's palace. There are many myths told about the Doladgathor, including tales of how the mighty trees once walked around freely, not beholden to any one place or requiring their roots to remain under the ground. They were tricked by a mighty warlock into growing still, losing their mobility. They make the best portals of all the trees the elves have tried over the ages."

"What about the wood in the second set of pillars?" Sam asked, walking her way over to them. They seemed more alive. She was certain that if she reached out to touch them, they'd try to tell her *everything* about themselves.

"They're newer, as you can tell," Al said. "They were added only forty years ago, to support the front pillars, which are aging."

"Will the front pillars have to be replaced at some point?" Sam asked, surprised.

"Yes," Al said, "and possibly sooner rather than later. While the portal, itself, is eternal, its container is ephemeral. Portals made from the Doladgathor last the longest. I'm surprised that these have held up for as long as they have."

"What, since the portal was first consecrated?" Sam asked. That was only a little over one hundred years ago.

Al shook his head. "These pillars have formed portals for over five centuries."

"What, we got used pillars? For our portal?" Sam asked, slightly peeved.

"This isn't the only portal on the human plane," Al pointed out dryly. "There are many others. And this one isn't that populated."

That actually made Sam feel better. Not because she was stuck with managing a minor portal, but because it meant that her family really was as puffed up about their importance in the magical world as she'd suspected.

Sam nodded. Five centuries was a long time, particularly for wood that wasn't painted or protected.

Except by magic.

Sam refocused her attention on the mist constrained by the four pillars. Though it was tightly boxed in, it still felt to her as if it stretched out in all directions an infinite amount. She'd never stepped through the Choowe portal herself, though she suspected that both Grandma Starling and Morgan had.

Her senses told her that the step would be a long one. Not quite the walk through a hallway that she'd experienced going through one of Al's portals, or the quick step going through one of her own. It would be something in between.

The cold of the portal space, which was what the black mist represented, sank into her bones even though she stayed on her side of the threshold. Though that space had many worlds floating in it, like soap bubbles in water, it was still featureless.

A void that sucked at her soul.

It was an abyss that she stared into, that stared back at her.

Sam shook her head and took a step back. The purple lights dancing in the darkness had grown thicker again, buzzing with angry energy.

Al stood beside her. Though his face was mostly blank, he still had a tension in his shoulders.

"How long was I staring at the portal?" Sam asked, her knees and back suddenly complaining.

"Long enough," Al said. "We should go now."

"My mother says that I'll lose myself in the portal,

someday," Sam said. Her voice had a faraway tone to it, almost as if someone else were speaking.

"We'll just have to make sure that doesn't happen," Al said. He indicated again that they should leave, walk through the door.

Sam nodded and turned away from the portal, though it still sang to her soul.

She wouldn't just walk into the portal with no destination in mind, abandon herself to it.

That would mean her mother would have been right.

And Sam wasn't about to let that happen. No matter how tempting just stepping into the portal and letting it absorb her might be.

AL INSISTED that they go back to her condo immediately, instead of spending more time at the mansion. It was almost as if he was afraid for her to spend a lot more time out there.

With the portal.

Once they left the portal room, Sam realized that she'd been staring into the mist for at least an hour and a half. Maybe longer.

That wasn't good. So she let him persuade her. They used the portal she'd created the night before, going from the kitchen of the mansion to the living room of her condo.

They spent a quiet night there, with Sam plowing through the first book, the compendium of portals, then starting on the next, the bestiary that Al had picked out for her.

The next morning, Sam and Al went back to the mansion early so that Sam could get upstairs and take a look around before her mother or Aunt Karen arrived.

Al went back to the portal room. Evidently, that was where he spent most of his time, when he wasn't outside communing with the trees. He'd stated that he'd frequently been sent to the elven plane when Grandma Starling had business, which was one of the reasons why Sam hadn't ever met him before.

It still seemed strange to her that he couldn't enter the portal room without her, but he could leave it at any time.

Hopefully he'd come find her when he needed a potty break and wanted back in.

The second floor of the mansion was organized similarly to the downstairs. The room directly above the portal was separated from the rest of the rooms upstairs by a narrow hallway that went all the way around the house.

The center room had been Grandma Starling's.

Sam could count the number of times she'd been in that room on the fingers of one hand.

The staircase leading to the second floor went straight up, no curves or landings. Sam deliberately walked on the edges of the steps, bouncing a little on her toes, listening to whatever creaks the wooden risers might give.

While the faded green carpet tacked to the center of the stairs was pretty threadbare, the stairs themselves seemed solid. Sam gave a sigh of relief when she reached the top. Chances were, she wouldn't have to do any structural work to the staircase when she refreshed the other rooms in the mansion.

She'd probably just tear up the carpet and refinish

the wood. And she might be able to do some of that with magic…

Upstairs, bedrooms lined one side of the squared off hallway. They were mostly separate, though a couple had inner doors that joined the rooms. In addition, there were a couple of large bathrooms—none of the bedrooms had an en suite bathroom.

Sam walked all the way along the hallway, circling the upstairs clockwise, opening up the doors to all the exterior rooms as she went.

Sheets covered the furniture in most of them, keeping the dust off. All of them smelled musty. Sam remembered arriving early for the holidays as a kid and helping her mother set up the rooms for the rest of the relatives.

There was just so much space! Sam didn't need it. She was used to her seven hundred square foot condo.

However, there was only a gardener's shed out back. No real workroom. Maybe she could transform one or more of the rooms upstairs into a studio…

As Sam walked, she realized that the single interior room, her grandmother's bedroom, while it had no windows, had at least half a dozen doors leading out of it into the hallway.

It was strange that she'd never noticed that before. Had she just never paid attention? Or had some of those doors been hidden?

Finally, after Sam returned to the staircase, she was ready to go into Grandma Starling's bedroom. She chose the door closest to the stairs, figuring that it would be a working door.

The room was dark and not only smelled musty, but sour, like vinegar gone bad. The air was chilly enough that goosebumps raised up all along Sam's upper arms.

The light switch next to the door turned on a chandelier hanging directly in the center of the room.

God, that thing was ugly. Rectangles of yellowed glass hung down in three tiers from it, like a cheap party hat. And it barely lit up the space despite its hulky size.

Directly under the light stood Grandma Starling's bed. At least that was pretty, if old fashioned. It was a four poster bed, and it had fine white netting draped over it, enclosing the space, like from a romantic painting. The posts were carved out of a dark wood, with smooth sides and fancy crown tops. Sam would bet that it was at least a hundred years old. The head- and footboard were similarly carved, with a repeating abstract pattern of notches in the wood.

As Sam stepped closer, she shivered when she realized that the bed was directly over the portal downstairs. She could feel it, a soft heart beating beneath her feet.

Would it be easy to sleep in that bed? Having the portal so close?

Or would sleeping above the portal leave her with nightmares of feeling trapped?

A sliver of magic was woven into the delicate netting that hung down from the four posts. Sam had no idea what it did, though she felt a slight spark when she ran her fingers across the surprisingly smooth fabric.

Would Al know? She doubted it. Morgan, too, was likely to be clueless.

Sam would just have to lie down on the bed at some point and experience it herself.

She wasn't looking forward to turning herself into a lab rat, that was for damned sure.

The bed dominated the bedroom, just as the portal took over the room below. Could Sam replace the bed with her own birds-eye maple frame? Possibly. That thought cheered her up immensely.

She looked around the rest of the room. There were cupboards for clothes, shelves for books, and an antique roll-top desk tucked into one corner.

And there was the chair that Sam had always seen downstairs, that used to be in the portal room. It was a tall wingback chair, upholstered in a faded green, gold, and red paisley pattern. Why was it up here? It was tucked in next to one of the cupboards. It obviously didn't belong there, as the end table beside it stuck out over one of the arms, making it hard to sit in.

Strange.

Sam knew that her family would expect her to take this room as her bedroom. But it was airless, had no bathroom, and in general, gave her the creeps.

She didn't want to stay there, that was for certain. Not with the room in its current state.

What could she do to make it better?

The wall of the room closest to the stairs was mostly taken up with a large fireplace. Sam would bet that it sat right on top of the fireplace downstairs, that the two fireplaces shared the chimney stack. Like downstairs, the wood grate had been replaced with a gas burner. Dark brown wood that matched the bed made up the mantle.

More pictures sat on top of it, but these were much older, pictures of Grandma Starling when she'd been a girl, of her two brothers and other sister (all long since dead), pictures of Grandpa Starling and his siblings, old photos of houses and places that Sam didn't know of.

Built in cupboards took up much of the wall opposite the fireplace. The other two walls were more clear.

Sam paused for a moment, then went out of one of the doors on the northern wall. Yes, she was remembering correctly. There was a bathroom there, and given the state of it, had probably been the one that her grandmother had used most of the time.

Sam walked along the hallway, rapping her knuckles along the interior wall. She would have to get a structural engineer to look at it, but she'd bet that at least some of that wall wasn't loadbearing.

Oh, her mother was going to throw a fit when Sam made changes to the mansion. However, if Sam was going to live here, it had to be comfortable for *her*. Not for her mother.

So, what would happen if she took out that entire northern wall of the bedroom, as well as the wall opposite it, and annexed the two bedrooms and bathroom there? She'd double the size of her bedroom, have space that wasn't just for sleeping but could be used as a studio, and have an en suite bathroom.

It would be a lot of work. Sam would get tired of living in a construction zone. However, it would make the space a lot more workable, at least for her. And she'd have windows, too.

Before Sam could get much further along in her

planning, she felt her mother arrive, along with Aunt Karen.

Sam wasn't about to tell them of her plans. Not yet. But if this was really her house, then she was going to do what she liked to it.

They could all just suck it.

SEVENTEEN

GOING through Grandma Starling's belongings went a lot more smoothly than Sam had anticipated. Both her mother and her aunt were focused on getting through everything as opposed to haranguing Sam.

There hadn't been that much in the way of jewelry. Sam had never worn much jewelry herself after she'd started working in the shop. Couldn't wear rings and swing a hammer. Necklaces were always hidden under her T-shirts. Though she had pierced ears, she hadn't bothered with earrings for years.

Still, Sam did take one piece for herself—a beautiful charm bracelet made out of sterling silver. Many of the charms had tiny pieces that moved, like the little jack-in-the-box that popped up, a book of matches that opened and closed, a door knocker where the knocker part swung up and down (and tiny words on it, *Knock Knock* across the top and *Who's There* at the bottom), plus a well with a miniature bucket and a handle that turned (though the bucket stayed in place and didn't go up and down).

Part of why Sam wanted to keep the charm bracelet was because it was so whimsical. It didn't fit her image of her grandmother at all. It was a reminder to herself that everything (and every person) wasn't always as they seemed. While she wouldn't wear the bracelet, she would ensure that it hung prominently over the dresser, so she'd see it frequently.

Grandma Starling's clothes were all going to a women's shelter, along with the toiletries. No one tried to talk Sam into keeping any of them, for which she was grateful.

Neither her mother or her aunt had any clue as to why her grandmother's chair was upstairs in the bedroom, though her mother did admit that it was odd.

After they'd gone, Sam went and found Al. He was sitting in the portal room, reading one of the non-human texts.

"Say, you wouldn't happen to know why my grandmother's chair, the one that was always down here, is upstairs in her bedroom, would you?" Sam asked.

Al shook his head. "No. I thought she'd gotten rid of it, along with the pedestrian sofa and light that used to be kept in here."

Sam didn't comment on Al's opinion of her grandmother's furniture, as she might have had the same thoughts about it.

"How did she get it upstairs?" Sam said, looking around. She couldn't imagine her ninety-two year old grandmother hefting that chair up the stairs.

"She must have created a portal just outside the door to get it up there," Al said.

"Why not just create another portal in here?" Sam said.

Al looked vaguely horrified. "No, you can't do that. You cannot create another portal in this room."

"Why not?"

"The easiest way to explain it is that the two portals would battle for dominance," Al said. "Though that's a simplification. One portal would try to subsume the other. The end result is that both would break."

That didn't make any sense to Sam. "But you can stack portals practically one on top of the other," she said. "That happens all the time out in the mudroom."

"Those are all temporary portals," Al said. "No, a working portal, like the Choowe portal, wouldn't tolerate another portal in the same room. It would try to suck all the power out of any other portal that was created here."

Sam glanced at the portal. That still didn't make any sense to Sam. Al was wrong.

Or maybe…Al was right, but was assigning things incorrectly.

He was just a protector. He wasn't a portal keeper, didn't feel the portal in his blood, not like she did.

It wasn't the portal that was jealous. The arches and the columns couldn't care less about anything else in here. No, it was the mist contained inside the portal arches, the portal *space*, that was hungry. That abyss that was always going to be trying to fill itself with more matter.

She didn't bother trying to explain that, though. It was just a feeling that she had. Maybe Al had centuries of study that he could point to that would prove her wrong.

And it didn't really matter, did it? It wasn't as if she were about to test his theory. She believed him that portals wouldn't tolerate one another.

Al looked at her expectantly. "And?" he said after a bit.

"So what can you teach me today about the portal?" Sam asked brightly. "My brother won't be here for a few hours."

Al thought for a moment, then nodded. Out of some pocket of space (and really, Sam was going to ask about that spell at some point, get him to at least show her a text that contained that spell because it was going to be *so handy*) Al pulled a small maroon leather bag. It rattled softly when he shook it.

"What's that?" Sam asked.

Al gave her a superior look. "Portal sensitivity training devices." He spilled out a few of the items from the bag into his hand.

"Really?" Sam said, looking at them. "They sure look like marbles to me." Glass ones, with pretty colors swirling in the center of each, but still, just plain marbles, each about half an inch across.

"Really," Al said snootily.

Sam would swear that Al was teasing her, but she wasn't certain, as she didn't know him that well.

Al instructed Sam to stand with her back to the

portal as he rolled a marble across the threshold between the columns and into the black mist.

Sam needed to be able to tell him not only exactly when the marble crossed the line, but which of the archways it crossed, as well as when the mist had swallowed it. It appeared that the marble didn't immediately vanish when it was placed inside of the mist. Sam counted to five before a fast-moving marble disappeared.

Al didn't really know where the marbles went to—portal space, that in between place that existed between the floating worlds was his best guess.

Sam would bet the same, that there was no coming back for any of those beautiful marbles.

By the end of their training session, Sam was easily able to identify which archway Al rolled a marble through, as well as able to predict, based on speed, how long a marble would last.

"It doesn't matter what material you use for this sort of training," Al confessed after they finished. "The portal absorbs everything at the same rate, whether it's feathers or iron. What's important is the speed at which something enters the portal."

"Gotcha," Sam said. She found it easier to look away from the portal this morning. Was it familiarity breeding contempt? Or at least making her slightly immune? She didn't know.

All she knew was that until the urge to commune with the portal diminished, there was too good of a chance that she'd lose herself in it, and would lose her soul to the abyss.

EIGHTEEN

MORGAN at least showed up on time, stepping out of a portal he'd generated in the mudroom. He wore his usual fussy attire: a light brown jacket made out of corduroy with another of his obnoxious off-white turtlenecks. He had the same raven black hair as Sam, though his eyes were a soft brown, not dark like hers. The browns he wore were actually suited to him. However, she always thought they made him look even more stuck up, particularly with his usual look of snootiness. (Seriously, had he learned that particular expression from the Elves or something?"

Sam had to admit that she didn't know her brother that well. They'd never grown close as adults, or learned to like each other as people. Sam had tried to overcome her resentment of him, as it wasn't his fault that their parents had always compared the two of them.

However, Morgan hadn't made the effort to get to know her either. He'd always been too tied up in his own world, his own family, his own importance.

His wife hadn't made it any easier. While Morgan may have called Sam stupid on more than one occasion when they'd been kids, his wife was dumber. Sam never knew what to talk about with her, usually just letting her blather on about the kids and the Goddess and whatever other nonsense was running through that empty mind of hers.

As Sam opened the door of the portal room for Morgan, he commented, "You've strengthened the wards on the door. Good."

"Thank you," Sam said, surprised to get any sort of compliment from him, even if he did sound slightly amused by her work.

Out of habit, she flicked the "switch" next to the door, bringing the lights up.

Morgan frowned at that. "You should learn to just do that with your thoughts instead of a physical gesture."

Sam shrugged. That was pretty far down on her list of things to do at this point. Plus, she wasn't certain she'd ever get good at directing magic without movement. She was a physical person who'd always worked with her hands.

"So what can you teach me about the portal today?" Sam asked as they walked over to it.

It still mesmerized her. She had to admit that.

When she looked back, Morgan stood there with his lips pinched together, giving her a disapproving look. "What has Alanthin been teaching you?"

"Why do you ask?" Sam said. She tried to keep the confrontational tone out of her voice. Probably didn't succeed, though.

"So I don't end up repeating lessons that you've already learned," Morgan said slowly, as if explaining to his five-year-old. "Since *you're* the one who's limited our time together."

"I don't trust you," Sam admitted easily. "That machine was too convenient."

"The machine that you destroyed? I had just bought it, you know."

Sam snorted in disbelief.

"I had. Grandma Starling asked me to buy it. She knew that she was failing. She wanted to start sharing her power sooner rather than later," Morgan said smoothly.

Too smoothly.

It was obviously a lie he'd rehearsed.

"I don't believe you," Sam said. "You'd had that machine for a while. Had used it, too."

"You can believe what you like," Morgan said coldly. "I know the truth. As does Mom. And Aunt Karen."

Sam gave a frustrated sigh, then deliberately rolled her shoulders, trying to release some of her tension.

Until she had some proof that Morgan had become a warlock, there wasn't much she could do.

Though she had no idea what she, or the family, would do if she found proof.

She held up her hand before the too familiar argument with her brother could continue. "Just...teach me something. That's what you're here to do."

Morgan looked as frustrated as she felt, wanting to protest his innocence more. Then he nodded and looked down for a moment, obviously composing himself.

"One of the advantages of a working portal is that the other end of it is fixed," he said as he looked up, easily falling into lecture mode. "A person passing through a working portal doesn't have to have been to that place in order to travel there."

Sam nodded. She knew that, having already learned it in the first book she'd read.

"While this end is permanently fixed, the other end isn't," Morgan continued. "It can be shifted."

"What do you mean?" Sam asked, surprised. That hadn't been in anything she'd encountered at all. Al had never hinted at it either.

"There are actually three ends for the Dunham portal," Morgan said.

Sam considered correcting him, pointing out that it was the Choowe portal, but she didn't want them to go off on some tangent. Again.

"The primary one is outside the court of the high council. The secondary one is set close to where the wood elves live. The third is near the caves where the dark elves are."

"Really? So could any of them just activate their end of the portal and come through?" Sam didn't like the sound of that at all.

And why hadn't Al told her about that possibility? Why hadn't it been noted in the first book she'd read?

"No, this end has to be tweaked as well," Morgan said. "Keepers on both sides of the portal work together to get it realigned."

"Did you see Grandma Starling do this? Or were you trained to do this?" Sam had to ask.

Morgan nodded. "It's one of the things that Alanthin probably doesn't know about," he added hastily. "As far as he's concerned, this portal has one and only one end."

"Why would Grandma Starling meet with the dark elves?" Sam said. "I thought they were decidedly unfriendly to humans." At least according to the bestiary she'd started going through. She'd skipped ahead to the parts about the elves, wanting to learn more about Al and his kind.

The bestiary claimed that the elves were actually three distinct races, that they didn't intermarry not merely because of custom, but because they were different enough that they couldn't breed together. There was no such thing as a half-anything as far as the bestiary knew. No half-human/half-elf combinations, no half-wood or dark elves.

Morgan said, "The dark elves aren't that bad. They're actually quite reasonable. Grandma Starling would deal with them occasionally. Don't believe everything you read in the old bestiaries here in the library."

"Huh," was all that Sam had to say.

"You'll know when they come knocking," Morgan told her. "You'll be able to sense when the portal keeper on the other end wants access. Grandma Starling always could."

Sam rolled her eyes at his expression. Clearly, he doubted that she'd ever achieve that level of sensitivity.

She'd just have to show him, and everyone else, that

she was fully capable of being the Choowe portal keeper.

Regardless of what they thought, or even her own doubts.

NINETEEN

SAM AND MORGAN managed to get through most of their allotted two hours only squabbling a couple of times. Morgan did know more about the portal than anyone else in the family. He was able to talk to her about the people coming through, listing off names of dignitaries that she'd be expected to host.

Luckily, Sam's dyslexia made it easier for her to learn aurally. She retained most of what she heard, even the long, strange elven names.

Of course, Morgan wasn't impressed with her ability to remember things. Sam had the feeling that nothing she did, short of giving him the full keys to the kingdom, would satisfy him.

Strangely, he didn't know anything about the wood of the arches, though he did know that they'd have to be replaced eventually. "Probably in your lifetime," he added.

"Do you know anything about the process?" Sam asked. She had to admit that due to her former job, she was more interested in the construction of the portal than the workings of it, at least on some level.

Morgan shrugged. "The elves will carry over the wood and construct the new arches. The portal keeper will have to contain the portal space while they switch out the old columns for the new. If the portal keeper isn't prepared, well, portal space will rapidly expand, then contract, and the resulting explosion would probably replace this house with a large, deep crater."

Sam shivered. That, at least, appeared to be the truth. "Is that something you can help with? Or should I rely on Alanthin for that?" Sam said.

Morgan gave her a cold glare. "I hope and pray that by the time it's necessary, you won't have to rely on anyone."

Sam nearly rolled her eyes at that. Of course, that would be ideal.

She didn't live anywhere near ideal. No one did.

"I wouldn't be too worried about the portal itself," Morgan continued. "What it contains is more important."

Sam knew she shouldn't respond to his snooty tone. She couldn't help it, though.

"I would think that any workman would want to be familiar with their tools," she said. Okay, so maybe her response sounded just as snooty as his to her ears.

Morgan actually rolled his eyes at her. "Yes. Your *tool* is portal space, not the thing that contains it. It's like me, dealing with money. Getting bogged down in how coins are minted has nothing to do with how the economy actually works."

Sam opened her mouth then closed it again. He was wrong. She *knew* he was wrong.

Was he deliberately trying to misguide her? Or did he believe what he was saying?

"Time's up," Sam said after a few awkward moments of silent glaring between them.

Morgan turned to go, but then changed direction and walked to the fireplace instead.

Sam followed him. He was looking up at the representation of portal space above the mantle.

"Do you know anything about the tapestries in France, that are supposedly similar to this?" Sam asked.

Morgan nodded, not looking at her. "Those tapestries were supposed to form a sort of working portal that enabled a person to step through to another place. Not having an actual space to step into, some sort of archway, made the portal use far too much energy. Plus, the material wasn't sturdy enough, so the tapestries only lasted a few trips before they disintegrated."

He sighed then looked at her, giving her a soft, half-grin. "I guess you are right, in some ways, to be concerned about the material the portal is built out of."

Sam could have been knocked over with a feather. Her brother, actually admitting that she was right about something? She wouldn't have thought that possible.

"The concept behind the tapestries was more similar to this carving, though," Morgan continued before Sam had fully recovered.

"How so?"

"Instead of being tied to a single place, or even a

few well-defined ends, they tried to build connections with many worlds. I'll have to see if I can find you a picture sometime. The center was the primary end location. But all around the boarder were small circles, representing other realms that the keeper could connect the portal to."

"Huh," Sam said. "Did it work?"

Morgan gave a shrug. "Not really. The ties to the other worlds were too tenuous to be easily exploited."

"I do have a question," Sam said as she followed Morgan toward the door. "Any portal can be used to connect to the netherworlds, right? Not just working portals?" The big compendium of working portals had implied that, but hadn't gone into any details.

"Technically, that's correct. In practice, though, most witches don't have the knowledge or strength to connect to a separate plane. Even the strongest denizens of the netherworlds still struggle to form portals between the worlds," Morgan said.

Sam walked Morgan to the mudroom where he had a portal to take him back to wherever he'd come from that afternoon. They'd already established their next meeting time the following day.

"I'm glad you let me come and teach you today," Morgan said, his words and smile obviously forced.

Still, Sam had to admit it had been useful. "Thank you for coming," she said as graciously as she could.

Was it wrong that she wanted to spritz air purifier after he'd gone? Just to get the smarmy stink of him out of her house?

She thought about what he'd taught her that day.

Mostly, he had been useful, not trying to send her haring down useless rabbit holes. And as far as she could tell, almost everything he'd told her about the portal had been the truth.

Sam didn't know what Morgan's full game was. She still didn't trust him.

It was obvious, though, that he hadn't given up his ultimate goal, which was full control of the Choowe portal.

Probably over her dead body.

CHAPTER
TWENTY

THE NEXT MORNING, Sam stopped by the shop to let Juan and the guys know that she was unfortunately going to have to quit, in order to run the family business.

Ron allowed her to take a leave of absence instead, keeping the door open for her to return if things with her family didn't work out.

Sam was in tears most the drive back to Ravenswood.

The next few days passed in a blur. Sam used portals as much as she could to move her belongings from her beloved condo to the mansion.

She worked alone, of course. Al couldn't be bothered to dirty his manicured hands in such labor. She moved in the mornings, and had lessons with Morgan, then Al, every afternoon. Her evenings were spent reading as much as she could before she fell into bed, exhausted, the night passing by in a blink before she got up and started it all over again.

The kitchen was first, because that was easiest. There wasn't that much to move. She'd use Grandma Starling's silverware and plates, only bringing her collection of hand-made mugs, her coffee altar, and a few of her prized pots and pans.

The rest went onto the local swap app. So her kitchen emptied out quickly.

Next, Sam tackled the bedroom. Her own things made their way into one of the guest bedrooms upstairs, right next to the bathroom that Grandma Starling had used.

Before she could continue, she had to clean out Grandma Starling's space.

The morning had started cloudy and gray, and it hadn't stopped raining since she'd gotten up. It was as good a day as any to start working in the windowless room.

Sam had asked Al if he had any idea what sort of spells the netting around the bed held. He was clueless, though he did volunteer to come look at it that morning.

First thing Sam did was to prop open every door leading to the bedroom. Though the place didn't smell bad, there was a musty feeling to the room that tickled the back of her throat, making it feel as though she was always about to sneeze.

She had boxes ready for all of Grandma Starling's clothing. Aunt Karen had already claimed all of the jewelry that no one else wanted, planning on taking it to a consignment shop for resale.

Sam doubted that she'd see a penny of the money from that. Then again, she had to remind herself that she really didn't need it. It was fine for Aunt Karen to have it.

Though honestly, her aunt didn't need it either.

Maybe Sam would do something really rude and ask about the money anyway, saying that she planned on setting up some sort of trust fund for the grandkids, and their college funds.

Opening the doors to the room didn't improve the lighting. Sam still had to turn on the one overhead light, that ugly chandelier.

She needed to replace that before she'd be comfortable moving in here. Luckily, there were a couple of building salvage places she could take it to, including the one down in Enumclaw. Let someone else believe they had found a treasure. She still wasn't sure what she'd replace it with. Maybe a square, modern looking light that was full-spectrum, the kind used to encourage houseplants to grow.

Al followed her into the room and stood next to the bed, studying the net draped over the four posts. With a bit more light in the room, Sam could see a slight magical glimmer to it, as though it were bathed in moonlight.

"So what does it do?" Sam asked after Al had brushed both his fingertips across the surface of the net as well as the back of his hand.

Al glared at her, opened his mouth, then shut it again. "As I think I mentioned before, it won't be easy to identify the magical powers of this netting. Particularly since it wasn't made by humans or elves."

"Really?" Sam said, fascinated. "Who made it?"

Al shrugged. "Not really sure. Your grandmother had dealings with many different netherworld beings. She joked once about having a treasure trove of goodies hidden in the basement."

Sam blinked. "The basement? Really? It isn't finished." She recalled never wanting to go down there as a kid. Bare lightbulbs lit the space poorly. Concrete made up the floor only in the immediate vicinity of the stairs. The rest of the floor was merely pounded dirt.

"I'm sure she was just joking," Al said dismissively.

"I'm not," Sam said. She marched over to one of the walls of the bedroom and put her palm flat against it.

One of the things she'd learned was that while she had a good feel for the mansion, she could sense many more details if she was actually touching one of the walls. She didn't know if that was because she was such a tactile person or if she'd grow more attuned with the place the longer she lived there.

Sam cast her senses down the wall, into the basement, feeling along the spaces there. Now that she was thinking about it, why hadn't Grandma Starling ever finished the basement? Why had she left it such a creepy, foreboding place? It wasn't as if she couldn't have afforded it.

Grandma Starling had sometimes called the basement a root cellar. She'd kept her canned goods there. Sam remembered as a child going to the blueberry farm in Bellevue, then spending a day in Grandma's kitchen making blueberry preserves. As well as returning in late summer, when Grandma had bushel baskets of tomatoes, and canning tomatoes as well as making spaghetti sauce and canning that as well.

None of the kids had ever volunteered for the chore of climbing down the steep basement stairs to fetch something from there. The older cousins had teased the younger ones with tales of impossibly big spiders guarding the space.

No, the domain the kids always snuck into was the attic, which was a lot less scary.

Sam oriented her senses by finding the stairs first, then the canned goods that lined the wall at the bottom of them. After she'd gotten herself placed firmly, she crept along the dark hallway, seeking to learn the space.

It shouldn't have surprised her that the basement was set up similarly to the first and second floors, that was, with a hallway going along the exterior walls and an enclosed room in the center.

Sam inched her awareness through the space, finally finding the opening into the center room. The door there appeared to be heavily warded, as heavily warded as the door into the portal room itself.

Interesting.

Inside the room, Sam found heavy flares of magic. She wasn't sure exactly what was down there.

However, it appeared that yes, Grandma Starling did have a treasure trove.

Before Sam removed her hand from the wall, she sent her awareness up, into the attic.

It was the only floor in the mansion that didn't have the same configuration. Instead, it was a wide open space, lit by the gabled windows along all the sides. The sloping of the roof made the areas near the windows very low. It had been a mark of passage when, as a kid, you could no longer easily fit into those spaces.

As far as Sam could tell, nothing magical existed in the attic.

Maybe that was why Grandma Starling had never finished the basement. Telling the kids that they couldn't go down there would have only lit their curiosity. Instead, the attic had been the special place they could sneak into without permission.

Because the attic was safe.

Sam shook her head as she went to join Al.

"Yup," she said after a moment. "There's treasure in the basement. I'll show you later."

Al gave her a cool look before he nodded. "Very well." Then he reached out again to the netting, running the back of one hand against it.

"I have to remember that you weren't trained as a magician, so you don't necessarily understand why it's so difficult to ascertain the exact magical properties of an artifact," he said, starting off in lecture mode. "To enchant an item, you must use more than one spell, either woven or knotted together. In order to determine what an item is for, you must first separate out the different spells, then identify each. And even then, you might not fully understand what the item is for, particularly if the spells aren't of equal strength."

That made sense. And her lack of training was really going to be a disadvantage here. She had no idea what any of the spells might be, or how they went together.

"So first, you have to separate the magic from the

item, to see what you're dealing with," Al continued. He ran the back of his hand down the netting again.

Sam copied him, trying to get a feel for what was net versus what was magic.

It took her a few tries, with Al critiquing how deep or shallow she sent her senses. Finally, she was able to lift the magic up from the netting to get a good look at it.

To her, it appeared as a heavy hunk of blondish-brown hair that had been braided. Not with three simple strands, no, but at least twelve all woven together. Each one represented a different spell. And though the strands were uniform, they were made up of many separate threads that she instinctively knew could easily fray.

Sam tried to tug it apart, but the magic wouldn't hold. Her image of it vanished.

Frustrated, she pulled out a piece again. The same braided representation shone against her palm. However, this time, in addition to the blondish-brown strands, she found a darker one woven among them. It was easier to separate out that one.

However, she had no idea what it did. She knew so few spells. It was difficult for her to figure out what the form of this one took. Was it a hand? A rake? Some foreign implement that she had no knowledge of?

Al followed her movements, looking over her shoulder, then did the same with a hunk he grabbed in his own hands.

"Huh," was all he had to say at first.

Sam waited a few moments for further enlightenment.

"As I said, this netting wasn't created by either human or elvish hands. My best guess would be Clandesh, but I don't know for certain."

That meant nothing to Sam. Before she could point out, yet again, that he needed to explain more, Al continued.

"The Clandesh live in a nighttime realm," he said, dropping the magic and turning to face her. "Their magic frequently deals with dreams and things half-seen."

That made sense, since the netting was draped over Grandma Starling's bed.

"You can't assume that the color of that one strand means anything," Al continued after a moment. "Some of the spells that look the blackest actually have very good results. And by 'good' I mean the opposite of evil."

"Point taken," Sam said. "But still, were you able to figure out what that strand did?"

"Sort of," Al said. He looked frustrated. "I believe it's a binding. It ties the user of the artifact to the item, growing stronger over time."

"Anything else?" Sam prompted after a bit.

"Yes. All artifacts need a constant supply of magic to keep them enchanted. You can't just create an item and forget about it. An item that is not constantly fed magic will lose the spells attached to it."

Sam nodded. She did know that.

"This net is powered by the portal below it. I believe that part of its function was to infuse the sleeper with a portion of the power that it siphoned off. This net, in effect, kept your grandmother young and strong, magically speaking."

"Huh," was all that Sam had to say. "So I shouldn't move it away from the portal, but start using it myself?"

"Not necessarily," Al said. "There's that binding that's woven into the net. That darker strand. Once you start using it, you'll become dependent on it. It will be harder and harder for you to regain your strength on your own, away from the net. It's possible that your grandmother became addicted to using this net after a while."

A horrible thought struck Sam. From the look on Al's face, the same one had occurred to him.

"So, by moving my grandmother to a hospital, away from her own bed, my mother may have killed her?" Sam had to ask.

Al pressed his lips together as if he didn't want to reply. But he said the words anyway. "It may have hastened her ending, yes. She did go downhill rapidly after she'd been removed from the mansion."

"Wouldn't my mother have known that?" Sam said.

"Not necessarily," Al said, shaking his head. "Your grandmother wasn't forthcoming about her powers or the magic she used. Plus, she *was* failing. Her body was growing old. Even if she'd been allowed to stay here, to sleep in her own bed, there's no guarantee that she wouldn't have died shortly anyway."

"Okay," Sam said, clutching at what relief Al was throwing to her. She didn't want to believe that her mother had been complicit in her own mother's death.

Or worse, her brother.

"Did Grandma Starling know about the binding spell in the netting?" Sam said after a moment.

"Probably," Al said. "The Clandesh are fairly neutral when it comes to other netherworld peoples. They wouldn't necessarily have tried to trick her or hide the consequences."

"I wonder when she got it?" Sam said. She felt certain that her grandmother would never have knowingly used such a crutch, not until she absolutely had to.

A new thought struck her. She remembered immediately after Grandpa Starling had died and how her grandmother had gone through such a difficult time. Not that her grandmother would have admitted to that. However, Sam remembered how pale and wan Grandma Starling had gotten. Had she complained at that time about not sleeping well? Sam had a vague memory of that.

If Sam had to guess, she would bet that Grandma Starling hadn't started using this net until after the death of her husband.

Sam considered the net for a while. She wasn't about to sleep under it.

Al appeared to be reading her thoughts. "I wouldn't get rid of this net," he said. "There may come a time when you've been drained, or injured. Sleeping under it for one or two nights would help you recover more quickly, without becoming dependent on it."

"But it needs to stay here, right?" Sam said. "Maybe folded into a box kept on top of the portal?"

Al nodded. "Yes. That way it will continued to be powered by the portal. Or else put in the basement, if the enchanted items down there are also getting power that way."

"That would be ideal," Sam said. She paused, then asked, "Is there an expert I can hire? Someone who specializes in determining the nature of enchanted items?"

Al made a face as if she'd just passed a particularly obnoxious fart. He still replied, "I believe so. Let me make some inquires."

While Sam wasn't about to allow anyone free access to the basement and the goodies hidden down there, not until she'd looked through them, having someone else to help out in the areas she wasn't good at only made sense.

"Thank you," Sam said as Al turned to go.

"You're welcome," Al said. He paused, giving her a look. "Thank you for letting me help you in this."

"You could help pack up stuff," Sam said to his retreating back.

Al didn't bother turning around, just waving a negligent hand in the air, as if to say that such matters were far beneath him.

Sam sighed and looked back into the room.

One mystery down.

Nine hundred and ninety-nine left to go.

TWENTY-ONE

PACKING up Grandma Starling's clothing went quickly. Sam shoved all the boxes into a portal that went directly downstairs, opening up next to the front door. From there, when she was ready, she'd open up a second one that went from the door to the back of her Jeep, making it even easier to load it up.

Once the dressers were emptied, along with the shelves, Sam stood for a moment looking around the room, trying to decide what was next.

May as well see if she could solve a mystery on her own, namely, why Grandma Starling had moved her chair from the portal room to her bedroom.

The winged back chair looked so out of place up here. Most of Grandma Starling's furniture was plain wood, carved, dark, and heavy, while the chair seemed almost ornate with its paisley pattern upholstery and much lighter-colored wood.

Sam freed the chair from where it was stuck, the seat tucked in under the table beside it. The first thing she checked was the legs. Had one broken or come loose, somehow?

But all the legs were still firmly attached to the base of the seat.

She pressed on the arms of the chair, slightly shaking it from side to side, to see if it had developed a wobble.

Nope. Solid.

Greatly puzzled, Sam slowly sat down in the seat.

Crinkle. Crinkle. Crinkle.

Sam shot out of the chair as if she'd accidentally sat on something wet.

Her butt was dry, as was the seat of the chair.

However, when she pressed her hands into the bottom cushion, that crinkling sound came again, as if it was made out of straw and not foam.

What the hell?

Sam removed the cushion from the chair. Turning it over, she saw that the zipper to hold the upholstered fabric together was undone.

With great trepidation, Sam slid her hand into the cushion. Her fingers touched paper.

Slowly, Sam pulled out pages that looked as though they'd been torn from a yellow legal pad.

Writing covered the fronts of each page, a very smooth cursive.

Grandma Starling's writing.

In the upper right hand corner a number had been added, so Sam could order the pages. Then she fired up the reading spell and dragged her finger across the first few lines. Her grandmother's voice filled the quiet room as the words rolled out.

> *I feel ridiculous writing this out, giving voice to my fears, then hiding the pages in what I hope is an obvious yet still hidden place.*
> *I'm assuming that I've passed, which is how you've stumbled upon these.*
> *If you, the reader, are Morgan Dunham, well, congratulations. You won.*
> *If you aren't Morgan Dunham, but perhaps Samantha or some other relative, heed my warning. Beware of Morgan Dunham. He didn't kill me, but he certainly hastened my end.*

Sam gasped and sat back.

She *knew* it! She knew that she couldn't trust her brother. Evidently, neither had Grandma Starling.

Was this the smoking gun? Could she use this as proof for her mother and the rest of the family, to show them that her brother wasn't to be trusted? Or would they put it down to her grandmother's failing mind and not heed her words?

It didn't matter. Sam was finally going to be able to forbid her brother access to the estate and the Choowe portal.

Should she go and find Al? Tell him the news? She hesitated. No, she had better read through everything first, then go find Al. She had no idea what her grand-

mother might say about the elf, and didn't want to accidentally cause him pain.

She read on.

Though Grandma Starling kept the door to the portal
room locked, it appeared that Morgan had figured out a
way of getting into the room without it notifying her.
The frustration in her voice was evident, as well as the
fear when, on more than one morning, she'd walked into
the portal room only to discover him there.

She even talked about how she couldn't bring this
up to anyone, particularly not Alanthin. In Grandma
Starling's opinion, the elves could never know that the
portal, as well as the portal keeper, were vulnerable.

Evidently, the reasoning behind that was obvious, as
she didn't bother to explain why.

It was the last page that Sam found particularly
chilling.

*I know that Morgan claims that he only wants to
help. But I suspect that he's found a way to
drain me, drain the portal itself, of power.
He's always been so greedy. Even as a
teenager, he was insincere in his care for me,
for the portal. All he craves is power.*

*I don't know how he's doing it. I think he must be
using a machine, because he doesn't have the
strength himself for those sorts of spells. I
haven't caught him in the act, though.*

Sam knew exactly what Morgan must have been

using—that damned machine that she'd destroyed. At least she didn't have to worry about that.

However, if Grandma Starling hadn't been able to figure out how Morgan was getting into the portal room, how could Sam? Particularly when she didn't have the experience or the sensitivity of the former portal keeper?

One of the first things Sam had done had been to strengthen the wards around the portal door. Morgan had even commented on it.

He hadn't seemed worried about it, though. That hadn't been the tenor of his words.

She thought back. Had he been amused by her attempt? Possibly.

So he wasn't getting into the portal room through the door. Al had said that any other portal created in the portal room would cause the portals to fight for dominance, as it were.

Was that how he was doing it? Creating a second portal in the room, which then drained the Choowe portal?

With great foreboding, Sam stood, focusing all her senses on the portal room beneath her feet.

Yes, that was exactly what Morgan had been doing. Draining the Choowe portal of its strength.

In fact, it was what he was doing right now.

TWENTY-TWO

SAM RACED down the stairs but hesitated before she blasted into the portal room.

Morgan was there. She could *feel* him, or at least whatever the hell was feeding off the Choowe portal.

Where was Al, though?

She knew that Grandma Starling had had reservations about the elf. However, he'd been the only one who'd supported Sam, who appeared to be on her side. And she *really* didn't want to face Morgan on her own.

Luckily, it wasn't difficult to track the elf down. He was doing that communing thing with the trees again.

Sam was shouting as soon as she spotted him. "Al! I need you in the portal room! NOW!"

It was gratifying how quickly Al heeded her call. She'd known from the bestiary that elves could run much faster than humans. He moved like a blur from the edge of the trees to beside her.

"Morgan's here. And he's attacking the portal. Come on!"

Sam rushed back into the house, throwing open the door of the portal room.

The sight that greeted her made her stomach churn.

Morgan hadn't opened a normal second portal. Instead, somehow, he'd opened up a portal in the representation of portal space that hung above the fireplace mantle. It looked like a beam of utter darkness that started from a pinprick on the carving, expanding to a three foot oval, attached to the abyss of portal space that the columns constrained.

"How is he doing that?" Sam asked Al.

"I don't know," the elf said grimly. "But you have to stop it. Before he drains all of the strength out of the Choowe portal."

"Any ideas how?" Sam said as she slowly approached the beam.

"Can you cut it off?" Al said, following beside her. "Shut down the portal?"

Sam looked at Al in disbelief. "I can do that?"

"In theory," Al said.

Sam raised one hand up toward the beam, jerking it back when it got too close. That cone of darkness was deadly. Anything put into its path would be instantly "disappeared" as it were, sent to the nether region of portal space, that abyss which still sucked at her soul.

Doing something clever like slipping a mirror into the beam so that it focused back on itself would just destroy the mirror.

No, she had to stop the beam at its source.

But how?

She walked over to the carving above the mantle. It

was supposedly a representation of portal space, and the netherworlds that floated in it.

Was the beam originating from one of those worlds? She had to assume so.

How to cut off access?

She couldn't close the Choowe portal. She didn't know how, and Al didn't have the time to teach her. Particularly since he wasn't exactly sure how to do it either.

Maybe she could close off the point where the beam was coming from, instead…

Carefully avoiding the sizzling beam, Sam lifted her hands to the base of the carving. Her stomach churned and fear spiked through her. All the hair along her arms raised up and goosebumps chased each other across her shoulders. This was worse than learning to blow glass, because at least then she'd had an instructor walking her through the process. As well as adequate protection.

Sam marshaled her scurrying thoughts, forcing her attention back on the problem in front of her. The magic shooting out from the carving felt foreign to her. It was not human, or even elvish. It tasted of long winters and crystalized snowflakes, bitterly cold places where the sun was weak and slept for months. For all the heat that the beam generated, the magic behind it was spiky and jagged, like broken ice.

Destroying the Choowe portal would create a tremendous explosion. Sam had believed Morgan when he said that, and Al had said something similar as well.

Destroying the carving that supported this beam would cause a similar sort of bang.

All Sam had to do was to close off that pinprick of power that was pouring through the wood.

While the magic was alien, and the beam was foreign to her, the *materials* that supported them were well known to her.

Sam understood wood.

She reached her senses up, skimming underneath the magical enchantments that floated on the surface of the piece, delving into materials beneath.

Though the wood didn't come from an earth tree, she could still follow the grain. Trace the life flow, where sap had once run. Inch her way up to the point of greatest magic, that pinprick of connection between this physical plane and somewhere else.

Slowly, carefully, Sam pushed her own magic into the carving. It was like trying to pour cold glue into a tight joint. Her magic didn't want to move, then it slopped over the sides.

Sam kept pushing, adding microscopic fractions of matter exactly where she wanted it to go.

It took time and skill to close the hole the beam shot out of. She had to be careful, or the edges of the wood would just singe away.

Fortunately, the wood of the carving responded to her. Layers accreted, like resin building up, until a solid block covered over the location from where the beam originated.

Abruptly, the beam died.

With shaking hands, Sam lifted the carved piece up, removing it from its resting place above the mantle. Al opened the door for her, and Sam continued going, through the mudroom, dropping the carving onto its face on the grass in the back yard.

If anyone tried to open up a beam again, it was going nowhere.

Sam took a deep breath. Her work wasn't done, and she knew it. Grimly, she went back into the room to look at the portal, at *her* portal.

It was failing.

The front pillars, the ones made out of Doladgathor, were weak. Their strength was almost all gone. In fact, she wasn't certain why they were still standing, why they hadn't collapsed to ash by now.

Had that been Morgan's plan all along? To destroy the portal, make the whole thing go boom? Killing her and Al in the process?

"That's not good," Al said, glancing at her, having come to the same assessment.

"I know," Sam said grimly. "How do I stop them from collapsing?"

"You can't," Al said. "Not in the long term. But if you can strengthen the front set, just for a short while. I can get a replacement here quickly."

Sam knew, *knew*, what she had to do. She'd known from the start that it was going to come to this, that it had just been a matter of time.

She was going to have to delve into the wood of the Doladgathor columns.

Do what her mother had accused her of, and go in too deep.

Still, she tried to avoid it. She stood on the threshold, between the two front pillars. They were too far apart for her to touch both of them at once. She stretched her hands out, palms facing the columns, then pushed out concentrated streams of magic toward the failing wood.

It wasn't enough. The wood inside the pillars was already compromised. It was just a matter of minutes before they collapsed.

"I'm going in," Sam warned Al.

That was the only warning she gave.

She stepped to the pillar on her left. Though the two columns looked identical, that one felt a fraction more alive than the other.

Wrapping her arms around the pillar, Sam let her consciousness sink deeply into the wood. Her soul sighed in contentment as she went down.

Yes, this was where she belonged. Deep inside the portal. Deeper than anyone else had bothered to go for a long time, if ever.

Far too deep.

CHAPTER

TWENTY-THREE

Though Sam knew she was still standing in the portal room, still had her arms wrapped around one of the pillars of the Choowe portal, still felt the warm hardness of the wood underneath her cheek, a part of her was now…elsewhere.

Sam looked up as she stepped back in this other room. A huge vaulted ceiling spread above her. It was all carved wood, a honey-rich gold color. The geometric pattern seemed vaguely familiar, though at the same time, Sam knew she'd never seen it before. It looked like a series of smaller cells encased in raised wooden panes. Some were square, others were hexagonal or even octagonal.

It reminded her of the organic structure of wood, when looked at under a microscope.

No nails or glue held those pieces together. No, they'd been carefully grooved, carved to perfectly fit together. Sam didn't know how she knew, but she did. Though it had an organic quality to it, every single cell had been painstakingly planned out, so the pieces fitted together exactly, into a solid whole.

A series of fluted pillars supported the carved ceiling, reminiscent of the pillars that made up the front half of her portal, that same burly oak.

Sam took another step away from the pillar she'd been hugging. Everything in this grand hall appeared to be carved out of wood. Something that looked like pale beechwood made up the broad floorboards, while the walls were heavy cedar logs. The air smelled like freshly cut pine. No windows marred the space, instead, the wood itself had a slight glow to it.

Sam took another step toward the center of the room, finally seeing the door at the far edge. She felt drawn toward that door, made out of thick slabs of dark oak, held together with grooves and wooden pegs.

A part of her recognized that stepping through the door would draw her even further into the wood of the pillars, another step away from the earthly plane.

Would she be able to return if she actually went through that door?

Sam didn't hesitate.

She had to go. It was either that, or turn around and go back now, let the portal be destroyed.

The door was solid, and it took all her strength to push it open.

When she stepped out, she was in a new world. A world she'd never been to. The sky might have still been blue, and the dirt beneath her feet brown.

Some sense, though, told her of the other-worldliness of it.

This was not her place, not where she belonged. There was a gut-wrenching sense of *otherness* that stiffened her spine, made her uneasy.

Was this how Al felt every single day he woke on the human plane?

Mist rose up around her, but Sam still took a step forward. Then another.

Except, she wasn't stepping. Not really. Moving, yes. Locomotion in a sense.

Sam was no longer herself. Maybe she should have figured that out sooner. However, instead of a human form, she was now a tree.

Her natural, true self, in a way.

The space around her cleared, the mists condensing into other tall forms.

Other trees.

Each of them was at least four foot in diameter. She had a hard time judging how tall they all were. Perhaps taller than a two-story house. The majority of the branches were up at the crown of the trees, forming a rat's nest of hair, as it were. Bronze serrated leaves, the length of her arm and in the shape of long blades, grew off both the branches as well as straight out of her trunk, hanging down in layers, like a thin blanket.

Sam suddenly understood the "burl" aspect of the wood. Those dark spots were where the stem of a leaf once attached.

The trees, all two dozen of them, moved as a group. Sam felt her front roots shoot out, dig into the dirt, then pull her trunk forward, while her back roots pushed her along.

It wasn't smooth. There was a lag between each forward movement. Then the jump forward felt abrupt.

However, she wasn't alone. All of the trees beside her were going through the same motions. They traveled in a roughly circular pod. The front trees would break the ground for a while, making it easier for all those who followed, then they would fall back and others would take their turn up front.

It didn't take long for Sam to realize that she, and all these other trees, were Doladgathor. She was on the elven plane, sometime in the past, reliving the dreams that the Doladgathor shared with her.

Though that wasn't the name they called themselves. Their own name, in their own tongue, couldn't really be pronounced by puny human or elven mouths.

Purple tinted the blue of the sky, making it look thick and warm, despite the fact that it was chilly, fall in the air and winter on its way. Green hills rose up in the distance, their grass cloaks shining like emeralds. When the group passed other trees they would bow their heads, amazed at the sight, the magic from the pod flowing over them and heightening their senses for a few moments. Birds accompanied them, working as heralds to announce the pod's coming.

Sam absorbed the language of the Doladgathor, though they didn't speak much.

It quickly became obvious where they were going. The pod had been invited to spend the winter with a rich councilmember, at their estate. They'd been promised exquisite soil in return for sharing their wisdom with all of the council.

Sam knew it was a trap. But she couldn't warn the pod away. Couldn't change the past.

When they arrived at the clearing, the first layers of the soil were as fertile as had been promised. The pod was tired after their travel, and sunk their roots in deep, resting as the red sun set, bringing on the velvet night.

The morning light painted a different picture. The Doladgathor were trapped. Under the initial layers was a thick pool of magic. Greedily, they'd drunk of it, poisoning themselves.

The magic had been laced with spells that froze their roots in place.

They could no longer move.

That didn't leave them defenseless, as the evil councilmembers quickly discovered. Anyone who approached the now stationary pod would be immediately attacked, filled with needle-sharp wooden darts which were long enough to pass all the way through a body, sticking out on both sides. Magical shields didn't stop the needles.

When the evil councilmembers came at the trees with fire, they discovered that the Doladgathor didn't burn like normal trees. Any fire thrown toward the pod, even massive fireballs, would be absorbed by the wood before it had a chance to do any damage. Lightning didn't work either, the magic sucked up by the Doladgathor, which they then used to strengthen themselves.

The only time an elf was allowed anywhere near the pod was when one of the trees passed away. Light would fade from the bark of the tree over the course of a week. Its bronze leaves would fall, leaving it naked though not shivering, not yet. The others in the pod would sing songs of their past, ballads of great thinkers, poets, and even warriors. Slowly the massive trunk would fold toward the ground, carried there by the pod.

After the trunk had lain on the ground at the feet of the others for a week, a group of respectful elves would be allowed to haul away the body of the fallen.

It didn't disturb the Doladgathor to know that their wood would be used by others. That had always been their way.

One by one, the trees of the pods fell. The winters were much colder without the trunks of the others to block them, the sun too warm without a neighbor's shade.

Sam resided in the last tree to go. Though the tree she lived in couldn't necessarily sense her presence, she still sang with it and tried to give comfort. It had never been alone before, but it still clung to life, the last of its kind. She wouldn't say that it was stubborn. That didn't feel right.

No, it endured, stoically, until the end.

Slowly, the light went out of the world. The nearby birds mourned. There was no one to catch them when they fell, the entire valley echoing with the sound as the trunk smacked into the ground.

Darkness enclosed Sam. She felt the tug of deep sleep, though she fought to stay awake. She couldn't die. She had to return to her world, to save her portal.

Slowly, light grew in the darkness. It took Sam a

few moments to realize that *she* was the light in the dark place.

All she heard was the mourning of the tree's soul that she'd shared, a whispering moan that sent shivers down her spine.

She reached out her hands to comfort the other being, to ease its pain and loneliness.

Ashes filled her palms, still smelling of wood.

But her right hand felt slightly heavier than her left.

Instead of dropping the ashes, she stirred through them, curious.

Three small nodules greeted her questing fingers. Each had a dull golden color, with a broad base and a slightly tufted top, like a beaked hazelnut.

Seeds of the Doladgathor.

Her throat closed with the sweetness of the parting gift from the tree she'd shared a lifetime with. She'd always assumed that it couldn't feel her, had no sense of her, but maybe it had. Maybe her efforts at comfort had been worth it.

Suddenly, Sam found herself in her own body again, standing in the hallway she'd originally come through, just inside the door. She stuffed the seeds into the front pocket of her jeans, hoping that they'd come with her back through the portal.

The walls of the hallway swayed. The ceiling trembled.

But Sam knew this wood, now. She'd spent enough time living inside of it. She reached out her hands and soothed the aches, plastering over the cracks, stabilizing the boards.

It wouldn't last. She knew that.

However, it would help the columns hold, at least for now.

Sam took one last long look at the vaulted ceiling, solid for the time being, memorizing what she could of the pattern.

She still didn't know what it represented, but knew that it was important.

Then she resumed her position, pressed tight up against one of the columns, arms wrapped firmly around it, cheek resting on the solid wood.

She didn't remember closing her eyes. When she opened them, she was in the portal room.

Al gave her a tremendous smile as she stepped away.

"You did it," he said.

Was that awe she heard in his voice? She hoped so. Her soul was weary with grief, with age, with mourning at the passing of those magnificent trees.

She looked at the columns. Yes, they were stable now.

They wouldn't last for very long. Maybe a day. Perhaps two.

However, they wouldn't explode at the slightest strain, destroying the portal and everything in the vicinity.

She took a deep breath.

Before she could ask Al about arranging for a replacement, Morgan stepped out of a pocket of darkness in the corner of the room.

Then raised his hands and *slammed* the front columns with powerful, dark magic.

TWENTY-FOUR

"No!" Sam screamed, racing toward her brother.

But it was too late. The damage was done.

The columns suddenly tilted to the side, all the power she'd granted them quickly drained away by the attack. An ominous creaking filled the room.

Sam came in low, body checking Morgan from the side, knocking him back on his ass.

From the shocked look on his face, he obviously hadn't been expecting a physical attack.

Dumbass.

Before he could recover and possibly turn his magic on her, Sam gave him a swift kick to the side.

Were those ribs she heard crunching? Good.

"Why are you doing this?" Sam had to ask before she went back to her beloved portal. "Is it because if you can't have the portal, no one can?"

Morgan gave a disdainful snort as he slowly pulled himself to a seated position, one hand cupped protectively over his ribs.

"All the power released by the portal will be absorbed by my traps," he snarled at her.

"You're a warlock. You only exist by sucking magic out of other creatures," Sam accused him, though he was no longer her primary focus. Her eyes were on the portal, assessing the damage, her mind racing, seeking an answer.

Nothing came to mind. She'd only been able to do superficial repairs to the wood. Now, the cracks went too deep, the structural damage too devastating.

"Duh," Morgan said dismissively. "And living as a live warlock is better than being a dead witch any day of the year."

Moving with almost elven speed, Morgan rose, turned, and fled through the dark space he had come from.

Al came over at that point and did something magical to close off the pocket. It involved a twisting motion of his hands, as if breaking twigs.

"I use these sorts of magical spaces for carrying my sword and other implements," he said. "I didn't know they could be used by people."

"Probably not by witches," Sam said with a grimace. "Only warlocks."

Al nodded.

Another loud creak made them both start.

The front pillars tilted further.

They'd go at any moment.

"We need to get out of here," Al said. He raised his hands as if to open a portal.

"No," Sam said. "We need to save the Choowe portal."

"How?" Al asked. "There's no time to bring in additional pillars."

"Then we shrink the portal back down to just two," Sam said. "There just needs to be a space to travel through." Sam had learned that in the first book she'd read. While working portals tended to have four pillars, that was a more modern construct. Earlier portals only had two.

Al grimaced at her. "Do you think you can contain the portal space?"

Sam shook her head as she moved over to the rear pillars. The cold abyss flickered between the straining wood, licking out with a freezing flame.

It yearned to be free of the constraints holding it.

Sam suddenly understood that a portion of whatever explosion that happened when a portal went boom was caused by the portal space greedily reaching out to encompass all the area that it could, sucking it back into its dark heart.

"Can you contain the space?" Sam asked. "While I reconfigure the pillars? So they'll take the weight?"

Al threw her a worried look. "Portal space has no weight."

Sam shook her head. "Stop being pedantic. Force, then. Energy. Whatever."

"I'll try," Al said. "But if you kill us both, when we could have escaped, I'm going to haunt you in the afterworld."

Sam didn't know if that was possible, but she wasn't about to argue at this point.

Instead, she walked up and wrapped her hands on the outside of one of the rear pillars.

The wood fought her. It wasn't anywhere near as welcoming as the Doladgathor. Then again, it had never gained true sentience. Awareness, yes. Anger, even, at those who had felled it, instead of allowing the tree to age with grace and only collecting it when it was done with the world.

She didn't have time to argue with it now. Particularly since it felt like trying to argue with an emo teenager.

"You're a wonderful specimen," she told the pillar, playing up to its vanity. "And while it may have been unfair, now, you have an important job to do. Saving the world."

All right, that may have been laying it on too thick.

The wood still hesitated.

Then the cold of portal space that Al was doing his best to restrain, reached out and licked it.

The pillar shivered under Sam's hands.

She felt its reluctant acceptance. Though it still despised its new form, it would help.

Particularly since now *it* would become the important part of the portal.

Sam nearly rolled her eyes at that.

Great. She was going to have deal with an immature portal personality.

Only if they managed to survive this.

Sam thanked the portal again, then spread her

awareness up and down, away from the spot where she touched the wood.

Though the archway was composed of a different wood, it had taken on the flavor of the pillars that supported it.

Except…now that Sam was looking at the wood of the archway from the inside, using her magical senses instead of just her eyes, she realized that it had taken on a honeycombed appearance. Instead of being composed of a single piece, it was shaped from multiple cells.

Sam's breath caught in her throat.

It was the same as the vaulted ceiling in the hallway she'd been taken to.

That was the basic structure of the portal. Those interlocking cells. No wonder it had felt familiar, though she'd never seen it before!

Sam focused on the archway, throwing as much of her strength there as she could.

A sharp pain in her side distracted her, made her look away, back into the portal room.

A black cloud floated a few feet away from her.

Sam knew, *knew* that Morgan was on the other side of that cloud.

It shot another dart at her.

Damn it! She had work to do.

None of those darts would kill her, she was certain of it.

They were just to distract her, possibly at a critical time.

She glanced over at Al, but he was completely focused on containing the portal space. His eyes glowed in concentration. The rest of his face had grown ashen, as though he'd been carved out of white oak. He held his arms out, his hands spread wide, as if holding a large ball.

Minor tremors shook his limbs.

He couldn't help. Not now.

Ow.

"Morgan, you're an asshole," Sam said out loud.

She immediately felt better for having said it.

Now, how to grow the archway?

In her mind's eye, Sam created a solid scaffolding, with a ladder-like support on either side and a wide walkway in between. Then she stepped up, onto the scaffolding, so that she could work on the archway between the two pillars.

Sharp darts bit her knees and ankles, but Sam ignored those as she focused on the work above her.

Raising her hands, Sam focused for a moment on the archway. She needed to strengthen it, if it was to support the full weight of the portal.

The honeycombed archway needed to be expanded, from about a foot wide to three feet.

In Sam's mind's eye, she saw the next piece of wood that was needed. It was triangular in shape, the center of it carved into a circle while the edges of it were grooved.

It took just a moment for her magic to form the shape of it, for her to feel it in her hand, taking up most of her palm.

Triumphantly, she slid the new piece in along the side of the skinny arch above her.

One down. Umpteen-million to go.

Sam worked as quickly as she could, walking back and forth on her scaffolding, grabbing and sliding in new pieces of wood. Her shoulders ached from the strain of reaching above her head. Her legs were on fire from the damned darts. She didn't dare look down, afraid that they'd look like pincushions at this point.

The wood started sticking as she neared the end, instead of sliding easily into place. She used her palms to hammer pieces into place, bruising them in the process. The skin along the edges of her fingers tore as she worked, her blood intermingling with the grooves. Splinters pricked her hands, deep wooden spikes that stung as she moved.

She still refused to stop.

Time took on an endless quality. She remembered once helping a friend grout a floor, the constant sweep of her arm as she troweled, then washed and cleaned. It had been constant physical labor for over twelve hours.

This felt similar, the familiar motions, her eye intuitively judging what the next piece needed to be, her magic creating it, and her hands attaching it.

The next damned dart finally struck her mid-waist.

Maybe Morgan had finally peeked into the portal room and seen that his cloud wasn't floating high enough to really do Sam any damage.

The next barrage of darts all flew to Sam's arms.

Damn it! She really did look like a pincushion.

She tried to banish the pain from her mind.

It was so hard to concentrate.

Just a few more pieces.

Blinded by pain, exhausted all the way through to her soul, Sam snagged the last few pieces that the archway needed.

She couldn't look away. Couldn't release her hold on the arch, or it would all come tumbling down. Couldn't blast that stupid annoying clod of Morgan's.

All she could do was work, the physical labor that she'd always prided herself about.

Three.

Two.

One.

Finally, the archway was complete.

Sam pushed what remained of her magic into the wood. Magic flowed out of her fingers into the portal itself. Sam gave everything she could, drawing on reserves that she didn't know she'd had.

The light started to dim. Still, Sam gave more. She didn't care if she drained herself completely, losing her life to the portal.

It had to stand. It had to survive.

She heard the change rather than felt it, a slight hum in the air, like a refrigerator cooling in the background. The pillars grew more rigid under her fingertips, the magic consolidating.

Was it working?

A gentle voice called her name. It took Sam a moment to realize that Al was trying to talk to her, to call her back.

With great effort, Sam pulled herself back, out of the wood, out of the portal, and back to the human plane.

Only two pillars still stood. Dust and ash marked the

place where the front two Doladgathor had once stood. A pang of sorrow went through Sam at the sight.

The rear two pillars—the only ones remaining—had lost their green hue. Instead, they'd taken on a reddish appearance, more like the arch that connected the pair of them. They'd grown thicker as well. Instead of being a foot in diameter, they were more like two and a half. The ornately carved crowns looked different now, less baroque, more straight lines.

The portal more resembled Sam in that aspect. She appreciated the cleanness of the carving.

Though she knew that inside, the spirit of the portal as it were, was still the same emo teenager that she'd have to deal with later.

"Ow!" Sam said as that damned cloud of Morgan's sent another dart, this time, striking her in between her shoulder blades.

Both Al and Sam turned and simultaneously sent a bolt of magic its direction.

The cloud shredded into thin threads of black that slowly disintegrated.

Finally, Sam took a deep breath and looked at Al. She had to grin at the appearance of him. His hair was mussed, his shirt looked wrinkled, and even his jacket had seen better days.

Then her attention was snagged again by the portal.

In between the two tall pillars the dark portal space flowed. It didn't seem as strong to her as it once had been. Maybe that was because it wasn't as thick. Purple squiggly lines still fizzed now and again in the darkness, along with the glowing golden dots.

Portal space, for all its greed, wasn't actually malevolent. It was thoughtless. It wanted to eat everything
because that was in its nature. It wasn't resentful now
that it was constrained to a smaller location.

Unlike her brother, who was still out there, still
ready to do her, and her portal, harm.

Then she swayed with exhaustion. She'd give so
much of herself to save the portal. Gone in too deep.

At least she'd found her way back out again.

This time.

"You're going to sleep beneath the netting upstairs,"
Al directed, taking her elbow and leading her out toward
the door.

Sam wanted to protest. She wanted to spend more
time with her creation, because she really did consider
the portal to be hers, now.

There would be time enough for that later, she
assured herself.

Time enough to explore the changes she'd wrought,
the strength she'd brought to the archway, the beauty of
the wood.

All the time in the world, now.

CHAPTER

TWENTY-FIVE

SAM STOOD under the trees beside the beginning of the driveway. Her mother and Aunt Karen stood beside her.

The day of Grandma Starling's memorial service had started rainy, but then grown nice, with a tender blue sky and dramatic white fluffy clouds.

Sam didn't know of any witch who was strong enough to affect the weather. However, it was perfect.

It had been a lovely service, and it had warmed Sam's heart to see Juan and the others. They hadn't known Grandma Starling, but they'd all shown up to support her. Roberta, the lawyer, had attended as well. Sam had agreed to a lunch date with her the following week.

During the week since the attack, Sam had shored up the defenses around the estate as well as in the portal room, removing all the hidden spells that Morgan had woven in there.

Though they both knew that technically they were breaking the rules, Al showed her the spell to beef up the magical boundaries that already existed in the land instead of insisting that she figure it out for herself.

While doing so, Sam had discovered one of Morgan's black ponds, as she'd taken to calling them.

Idiot had set it up so that it crossed over the border of the property. If it had lain along the edge of it, not crossing the boundary, it might have taken her a lot longer to find one of them.

Once she had a taste of one, though, she knew what to look for, and had made it her mission to destroy each and every one of them.

The one in front of her was the last one. She'd kept it as she'd found it, needing to show it to her relatives.

First, Sam crafted the spell she'd come up with for stripping the illusion from the magic. It took the form of an antique scraper, the kind used to remove paint and stain from wood, with a sharp metal top and a comfortable long wooden handle.

Though her mother and her aunt both didn't approve of how Sam physically moved her hand as if scraping away the illusion that hid the black pond, at least it got the job done.

The gasp they both gave was very gratifying.

"What is that thing?" Mom asked, recovering first.

"As far as I can tell, it's an energy trap, set by a warlock," Sam said. "Morgan created it, as well as the others. They were supposed to absorb the energy that shot out when the portal exploded."

Sam had told her family what had happened. She'd also shown them Grandma Starling's hidden notes.

While her mother had seemed inclined to believe

her, Aunt Karen had voraciously argued that Grandma Starling had been losing her mind, growing paranoid, that her precious nephew couldn't have done such damage, and so on.

Sam had been prepared for that, which was why they were all there, in front of the black pool.

"Does this magic seem familiar to you?" Sam asked when neither her mother or Aunt Karen responded.

Her mother pressed her lips together, but nodded. "It does. It's familial."

"Maybe you created it," Aunt Karen said, turning an accusing gaze at Sam.

Sam snorted at her. "So either I'm an imbecile with no magic at all, a savant who doesn't need to think when doing magic, or maybe I'm a super dark witch with enough power to also be a warlock? Are you kidding me?"

"I don't need to listen to this, or be treated this way," Aunt Karen said, marching off in a huff.

At least the blackberry bramble didn't appear to care for her much, as her skirt was snagged by thorns before she got very far. Cursing, she freed herself and continued on.

"Leave her," Mom said, before Sam could throw yet another sarcastic comment after her aunt.

"You believe me, though, right?" Sam said. She knew she shouldn't care. As the head of the family, Sam could make whatever decisions she deemed necessary for the safety of the portal.

Which included banning her brother from the estate for life.

He and his family had disappeared from their house. A real estate agent had been remotely hired to sell the property, and had signed quite a powerful NDA in the process as well.

Sure, maybe they could track where Morgan had gone through magical means. But it wasn't illegal to be a warlock.

Immoral as hell, but until he attacked again, Sam couldn't do anything about him.

Hunting him down and killing him like a mad dog wasn't her style, though she might have fantasized about it. Maybe. Once or twice.

"I do believe you," Mom said with a sigh. "I don't want to admit it, but it appears as though my son has turned himself into a warlock."

Sam wondered at the emotion in her mom's voice. Was that anger she heard? Regret? Guilt?

Before Sam could ask, Mom continued. "How do you get rid of this thing?"

Sam let the subject be changed and returned her attention back to the black pool in front of her. In her mind's eye, it glistened like an oil slick. It was about three feet long but only a foot wide, floating in midair like a heat-haze mirage.

It smelled of dark magic and sour apples, with a bitterness that proclaimed its dark intentions.

"I need to break the outline of it," Sam explained. "Once the side is pierced, the magic will flow out. It's an easy spell to break, because it looks like a pond, floating in midair, the shape is unnatural."

"Interesting," Mom said. "Please, show me?"

Sam nodded, flustered and cursing herself for feeling that way.

For once, Al hadn't shown her how to deal with the damned thing. She'd learned about it from one of the books she'd consumed that week, all about spells.

Disrupting the form, the shape that held the magic of a spell, was one of several ways to dispel the magic. For Sam, it was one of the easiest ways. She figured it was again related to how physical she was, as well as all the renovation work she'd done. If she could visualize the form, she knew how to break it apart.

Sam had actually crafted her own spell, in the shape of an icepick, that she used to prick the side of the black pool. It took the least amount of effort from her, which had been really important at the start of the week when she'd been recovering from her ordeal and unable to do much magic at all.

"What happens to the magic after you release it?" Mom asked, watching Sam critically as she broke the side of the black pond.

"It flows into the ground," Sam said. "After it's sifted through the dirt, I can use it to further strengthen the border around the property." She likened it to water being purified after traveling through an aquifer.

"Very good," Mom said, watching the black pool drip out the side.

Sam had learned early that she really just needed a pinprick. At first, the magic would slowly drip. Then, the hole would widen as the form weakened, the magic eventually gushing out like a waterfall.

The entire process took between three to four

minutes. The magic needed to be processed by the ground for a day before Sam could scoop it back up again.

"Well done," Mom said as the magic vanished from their sight.

Sam held herself still, as it seemed like her mother wanted to say more.

"I know I probably haven't said this to you often enough, but I am proud of you," Mom said. She looked up defiantly at Sam, as if daring her to argue. "You saved the portal. And the estate."

Sam nodded. It was...nice, she guessed, that her mother was finally acknowledging her as someone who was capable, and not just a tremendous disappointment.

It still felt like too little, too late.

"And I wanted you to know that I support you, in all the decisions you've made," Mom added as she turned to go, to walk back to the mansion.

"Thanks, I think," Sam said. She couldn't help it. She didn't point out that she honestly didn't need her mother's support.

She'd made the decision about Morgan, and all of them were just going to have to live with it.

Mom seemed to hear her commentary anyway. "It is important that I support you, you know," she said quietly. "So that the others don't begin to question your fitness."

The way that her mother said that filled Sam with unease. "What, is there a way to remove the portal keeper from the portal? If they're deemed unwell, mentally?"

"There is," Mom said, nodding. "But the family wouldn't do that to you," she added hastily. "No matter what Karen might say."

"Any idea why she still supports Morgan so much?" Sam asked.

"She's probably been listening to him for a decade or more complaining about how I'm mistreating him," Mom said with a wry smile.

"Really?" Sam said, shocked that her mother would say anything bad about her brother. Morgan had always been the golden one, the one who could do no wrong. She was the fuck-up, and had never been allowed to forget that.

"Really. I love my son. I love both my children," she hastily added. "That doesn't mean I don't also see their faults. Morgan has always had a greedy side that I tried my best to curb."

Sam suddenly realized that her mother blamed herself for Morgan becoming a warlock.

"Mom, it wasn't your fault," Sam said. "Don't try to take on his guilt or become some kind of martyr. He chose that path. You didn't force him down it."

Her mother shrugged, and Sam knew that no matter what she said, her mom was always going to feel guilty for how things turned out.

That she became the portal keeper, and her brother had turned to the dark arts.

"Morgan and his family are no longer welcome in my house either," Mom said firmly. "Not unless that dishrag of a wife also disappears."

Sam glanced over at her mom, incredulous. Really? Did her mother dislike Laureen as much as Sam did?

"I will miss seeing my grandchildren," her mother finally admitted. "But it might already be too late for them."

Sam nodded. Those three kids had always been hellions. Was it partly because their father had become a warlock, an oath breaker, and was no longer a witch?

"So, maybe it's time for you to consider settling down," Mom continued with an overly bright smile. "Find a husband. Raise some kids."

Sam opened her mouth and shut it again. Nope. Not happening anytime in the near future.

"You might want to give it some serious consideration," Mom added. "Who will be your heir? The heir to the Choowe portal?"

With that she walked away, probably pleased with herself that yet again she'd managed to completely disturb Sam's world.

TWENTY-SIX

AFTER EVERYONE HAD LEFT the memorial, Sam found Al standing out at the edge of the trees in the backyard, doing that communing thing he always did.

Long shadows crept across the grass behind them. The spring chill had deepened, and Sam knew she wouldn't want to stand out here for long.

Still, there was something she needed to do. And she wanted, well, if not Al's help, then maybe his blessing.

"There's no such thing as a half-elf," Al said as way of greeting. "No half-human hybrids with any of the beings from the netherworlds."

"But?" Sam prompted after a few moments when he didn't go on. "I can tell there's a 'but' coming up."

"But," Al said, throwing a sly grin her direction, "it still wouldn't surprise me to learn that you had some wood elf blood in you somewhere."

Sam gave him a warm smile in return. The arch that she'd constructed was holding the portal space nicely. So well, in fact, that the elves they'd brought in to consult hadn't thought that a second set of pillars was necessary.

Mother, of course, was livid. In her mind, the importance of the Choowe portal was diminished if the portal itself was smaller.

It was still just as magical, or at least that was what everyone had been telling Sam. She didn't really know, as she'd never had the time to become attuned with the old portal.

The new one she knew, probably better than anyone, including Al.

Al hadn't been the only one astonished at the work she'd done, particularly given that she was both a human as well as a very new portal keeper.

All Sam could point to as an explanation was that she had a very long history of building things and fitting them together just so.

Privately, she'd decided that ability was the answer to why the portal had chosen her for the next keeper. Though the magic wasn't sentient, it still was aware enough that it wanted to live, and it chose who it thought would be the strongest keeper, able to get it through having the new pillars put in.

Though maybe it had been the Doladgathor pillars who'd chosen her.

Sam would never know for certain. It might have just been luck of the draw—since Morgan wasn't available, as he'd become a warlock by the time Grandma Starling had died, the portal had chosen her instead.

Speaking of the Doladgathor…

Sam reached into the front pocket of her jeans and pulled out the seeds the Doladgathor had given her.

When she'd first brushed the ashes from them, they'd been a dull golden color, like a seed that had been weathered.

Al had been shocked when she'd showed them to him. He claimed that it was the most important gift that anyone had ever received.

Sam had refused to give him any, though. It had been the high elves who'd killed the Doladgathor in the first place.

Instead of planting the seeds right away, Sam had kept them in her pocket. They appeared to have been influenced by her warmth, as well as her magic, for now the seeds were a bright golden color. An opalescent sheen had developed across the shell as well. The tufts at the top were noticeably longer and fluffier, like tiny white feathers.

"I think they're ready," Sam said, holding the seeds out for Al to see them.

He shrugged. "You're the wood elf here," he teased, though his face remained solemn. "Where are you going to plant them?"

"I don't know," Sam said. "They're not human, or earthly trees. I have no idea what type of soil they like, if they need sunshine or shade, should I keep them moist or dry, nothing." Consulting her memories of living as the Doladgathor hadn't helped her either. Trees that could move hadn't been picky about any of that. If they needed more sun or shade they could just walk themselves over to the perfect spot, or even stroll over to a nearby river for a drink.

"Where does your heart tell you to plant them?" Al asked after a moment.

"Right here," Sam said. "These woods have always seemed a touch foreboding to me. I think that was in part because of how much of my brother's icky black pools were seeded out there, malevolently waiting."

"Do you need some help?" Al said as he moved to the side.

Sam shook her head, kneeling down on the damp dirt.

The smell of the mulch filled her nose. It brought memories that weren't hers, but of the Doladgathor, who'd shared what had felt like a lifetime with her, though it hadn't been more than a few minutes.

Sam let her soul guide her hand, and she planted the three seeds in a line at the edge of the woods, where the grass met the trees. She spaced them several feet apart from one another, so that they'd be close enough to support each other, while at the same time, far enough away that they'd have the room to grow broad and tall.

"Will they thrive here?" she asked Al after she stepped back, futilely brushing the dirt from her knees.

Al shook his head, then waved a hand negligently, her clothes instantly clean.

Damn it, she was going to have to figure out that spell sometime. Al refused to teach it to her. Probably because he enjoyed teasing her too much about how disheveled she looked, like a worker and not a proper witch.

Too bad. She was a working witch, not some grand lady who spent all her time with books and spells.

"I don't know if the trees will grow here, on the human plane," Al said finally. "I don't think the Doladgathor would have given you the seeds, though, if they'd believed the trees wouldn't be able to flourish here."

"They won't be mobile," Sam said. "There isn't enough magic in the air, in the land, anywhere, for them to be able to walk."

"I know," Al said. "They probably knew that as well. They just wanted to grow again. To continue to live, even if that life is very different from what they'd once known."

Sam had to nod at that. Her life was completely different than what it had once been. She was *important* now, in ways she'd never been before.

It was both ridiculous as well as slightly intimidating.

Tomorrow, the portal would officially be open again, and the first of her visitors would start to come through.

She knew that at some point, Morgan would be back. Hopefully she could have something of a breather first before the next crisis struck.

In the meanwhile, she was going to spend this evening back in the portal room, hanging out with Al, reading through some musty old tome while sipping tea with a touch of brandy in it.

Then sleeping upstairs, without the netting, and dreaming of what she'd build next.

READ MORE!

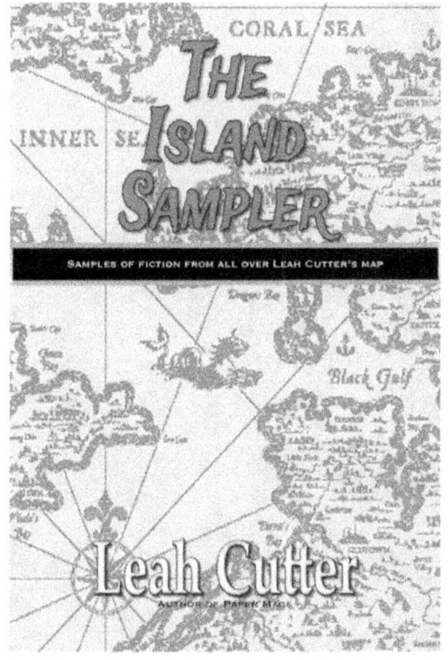

Do you enjoy exploring strange new worlds, new cultures, new people?

Journey into the various lands envisioned by Leah R Cutter.

About the Author

Leah R Cutter writes page-turning fiction in exotic locations, such as a magical New Orleans, the ancient Orient, Hungary, the Oregon coast, rural Kentucky, Seattle, Minneapolis, and many others.

She writes literary, fantasy, mystery, science fiction, and horror fiction. Her short fiction has been published in magazines like *Alfred Hitchcock's Mystery Magazine* and *Talebones*, anthologies like Fiction River, and on the web. Her long fiction has been published both by New York publishers as well as small presses.

Find Leah's books on Knotted Road Press at (www.KnottedRoadPress.com)

Follow her blog at www.LeahCutter.com.

Reviews

It's true. Reviews help me sell more books. If you've enjoyed this story, please consider leaving a review of it on your favorite site.

Come someplace new...

Do you enjoy exploring strange new worlds, new cultures, new people?

Journey into the various lands envisioned by Leah R Cutter.

Sign up for my newsletter and I'll start you on your travels with a free copy of my book, *The Island Sampler*.

I will never spam you or use your email for nefarious purposes. You can also unsubscribe at any time.

http://www.LeahCutter.com/newsletter/

ABOUT KNOTTED ROAD PRESS

Knotted Road Press publishes dynamic fiction set in exotic locations. Our authors cover a wide range of genres including science fiction, fantasy, mystery, literary, and poetry. We also have unique non-fiction voices in genres such as autobiography, business, cookbooks, and how-tos. We offer both DRM-free ebooks and print books for a global readership.

Knotted Road Press
www.KnottedRoadPress.com